the Sea Singer

the Sea Singer

craig moodie

ROARING BROOK PRESS
New Milford, Connecticut

Published by Roaring Brook Press
Roaring Brook Press is a division of Holtzbrinck Publishing
Holdings Limited Partnership
143 West Street, New Milford Connecticut 06776

Distributed in Canada by H. B. Fenn and Company Ltd.

Library of Congress Cataloging-in-Publication Data
Moodie, Craig.
The sea singer / Craig Moodie.— 1st ed.
p.   cm.
Summary: After his father and brothers fail to return from a voyage to
the west, Finn, a twelve-year-old Viking, stows away on Leif Ericsson's ship
and sails to North America to search for them.
ISBN-13: 978-1-59643-050-1
ISBN-10: 1-59643-050-8
[1. Seafaring life—Fiction. 2. Vikings—Fiction. 3. Fathers and sons—Fiction.
4. Ericson, Leif, d. ca. 1020—Fiction. 5. Adventure and adventurers—
Fiction. 6. North America—Discovery and exploration—Norse—Fiction.]
I. Title.

PZ7.M7723Se   2005
[Fic]—dc22   2004029995
Roaring Brook Press books are available for
special promotions and premiums.
For details contact: Director of Special Markets, Holtzbrinck Publishers.

First Edition August 2005
Book design by Michelle Gengaro-Kokmen
Printed in the United States of America
10 9 8 7 6 5 4 3 2 1

Alison Moodie Samph inspired this book
and I dedicate it to her as well as to Ellen,
Mary Rose, Matthew, and Salty

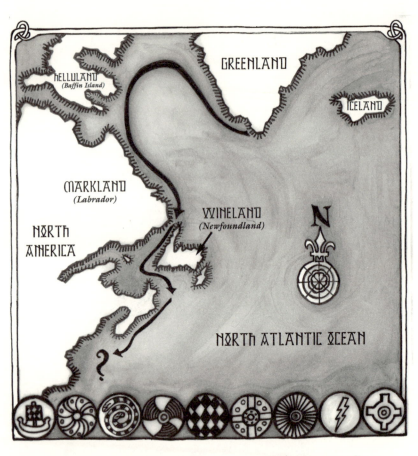

viking voyages to north america,
c. a.d. 1,000

auchor's noce

Several years before A.D. 1000, an Icelander named Bjarni Herjolfsson was blown off course while sailing his ship from Iceland to Greenland. After days lost at sea, he found himself off an unfamiliar coast, which he described to Leif Ericsson back in Greenland as covered in green forests. This was intriguing news to Leif. Wood was scarce in Greenland. The Vikings were always on the hunt for new sources of timber, grazing lands, and trade routes.

Leif set off on an expedition that retraced Bjarni's route in reverse past Baffin Island, Labrador, and Newfoundland, and may have extended as far south as Cape Cod. Landing on the shores Bjarni had described, he became the first European to set foot on North American soil—five hundred years before Columbus. He named it Wineland, or Vinland, for its abundant grapevines.

The Vinland sagas—*The Greenlanders' Saga and Eric the Red's Saga*—offer different versions of the Viking voyages of discovery and open the door to speculation about the nature of these gutsy, resourceful seafarers who braved the frigid North Atlantic in their sleek and resilient ships. It is in this spirit that I have plucked a few threads from these narratives and spun and twisted them into the tale you are about to read.

the Sea Singer

a sail on the horizon

Finn crawled through the coarse grass to the edge of the cliff and peered over. Far below, waves boiled and boomed against the rocks. Plumes of spray jetted into the air. Seabirds soared and cried. Beyond the rocks and the snow-white surf, the sea stretched before him. All he could see were the scattered islands called skerries ringed with white surf, the sea turning blue green where the sun broke through the clouds, a gleaming blue iceberg glinting in the sun, and the long thin line of the horizon.

What he wanted to see wasn't there. He came to the edge of the cliff every day to scan the sea for a sail, the sail of the ship that would bring his father and his two older brothers back from the land beyond the western sea.

Everything Finn knew about this distant land came from the stories his father and other Vikings told as they sat around the fire swapping yarns and drinking beer. It was a land of mystery, a land said to be rich with timber and teeming with wildlife, a land of strangeness, danger, beauty, and bounty.

Once a man who had seen this land with his own eyes had sailed to the village. His name was Bjarni Herjolfsson, and he'd described the route he'd taken. Listening in the shadows that night as Bjarni told Finn's father, mother, and brothers of the distant waters and shores, Finn's eyes had sparkled with firelight and excitement.

When Finn imagined this place, he saw the dense woods of the stories. And he saw something else: a shadowy human figure emerging from the trees to squat beside a pond for a drink of water. He could not make out the face of this person, but he sensed that the figure had something to show him. As many times as he pictured the woods, he saw the figure. Just what this shadowy presence meant remained a mystery to him.

He scanned the horizon again. Today was no different from the other days. There was no sail. Never could he see far enough. He wanted to know what lay beyond the bowstring-thin horizon. What could help him see?

He moved back from the cliff edge and sat on a boulder. He heard the bleating of the sheep behind him. Sheep, he thought. Stupid sheep. More likely to go after a tuft of thorn on a cliffside and risk tumbling hundreds of feet into the breakers than to crop the sweet grass on the gentle slopes.

He did not take his eyes off the sea. He let the immensity of the world absorb him. The great headlands stretched away on either side of him, rent by long, deep fjords fed by dashing streams. The mountains towered behind him, their glaciers glittering in the silver light right up to the gleaming Ice Cap. Shreds of white clouds chased their shadows past him.

He closed his eyes and turned his face to the sun. He let the sun glow pink-red through his eyelids. Maybe this was the way to see: Look inward. The moment he closed his eyes the forests of Wineland appeared to him again. And there was the figure, moving out of the woods to the pond. If only he could get closer to the figure, maybe he could find out what he was meant to see.

A sheep bleated again.

"Oh be quiet," he said, his eyes snapping open. The wind caught the words and carried them away. "Why don't you take care of yourselves?" His long yellow hair swirled into his eyes. He thrust it aside.

Finn wanted to go voyaging with his father, not tend to the family flock. He was in his twelfth summer and he knew that when his father returned, he would set sail with him to trade their woolens in distant lands, to search for new sources of food and timber, to ride the wind in *Dragonwing*. Maybe, just maybe, his father would set a return course to the land to the west. Maybe he could crew with his brothers aboard his father's dashing ship, sailing over the shining back of the sea to find great treasure and adventure.

As a gull passed before him, a thought came to him: If he were that gull, he would soar high enough to see *Dragonwing* out at sea. He would catch the wind and fly away.

He watched the gull rise with an updraft from the breakers below and hang as if weightless against the sky.

He looked at the small spear that he carried with him. Its point was covered with a flap of leather so he wouldn't hurt himself or anything else. His brother Einar loved to needle him by saying, "Where can I get a flap like that?" He knew that if his father had returned last season he would already have his real spear, a real knife, a real bow and arrows, not this child's toy. But his mother didn't understand. She told him it was up to his father to decide when he was ready to carry real weapons.

The short season of voyages would soon pass its peak. Ships were making their passage from the settlements of Greenland to Iceland and Norway to trade skins of all kinds—polar bear, fox, musk ox, goat, sheep, caribou, seal—and tusks of walrus and rope made of walrus skin. Other ships from Iceland and Norway arrived with timber and iron. A few intrepid Greenlanders embarked on voyages to find the land to the west.

The snow had melted long ago, and the ducks and geese had flown north to lay their eggs and raise their young. The light touched the sky at every hour. But his father, his eldest brother Gunnar, and Einar had not returned.

He saw Gunnar before him, Gunnar the tall, dark-haired one with the long face and distant eyes, Gunnar, who had had the patience to teach Finn to play hneftafl, or chess, even though Finn quickly learned to beat him. Finn had carved an ivory warrior chess piece out of a walrus tusk in gratitude for Gunnar's instruction. Gunnar drilled a small hole in it, strung a leather cord through it, and wore it around his neck for good luck.

He saw Einar before him, the jovial one with a hornet's temper, a freckled bear with a wispy red beard that Gunnar called "duckling down."

And he saw his father Olaf with his ruddy face and eyes the translucent blue green of a summer iceberg. He could practically feel the bristles of his fox-colored beard and his callused hand gripping his shoulder in greeting.

And he could feel the steady grip of his father's hand on his shoulder as he said, "Finn, I am counting on you. Your mother will have only you to depend on while we're a-viking. You are becoming a man, Finn, and a man carries out his duties."

He blinked and looked out at the empty sea and did

not want to think about what might have happened to his father's ship. Many times ships set sail, never to be heard of again. There were storms and whirlpools. Sea monsters, so some people said, roamed the open waters, and sometimes sank Viking vessels.

And he'd heard tales of Skraelings, hostile people who lurked in the dense, shadowy stands of spruce and fir in the land to the west, ready to attack anyone who trespassed on their shores.

Finn wondered what he would do if he met a Skraeling. He pictured himself drawing a sword and holding it high. He imagined the Skraeling running away, terrified of his swishing blade.

But the figure emerging from the woods in his imagination: It must be a Skraeling. And if it was, what then? If he scared it away, he would never find out what the figure was meant to show him. Maybe attacking first was not so wise.

Finn picked up his stick and turned to go. As strong as his wish to handle real weapons and set sail was his need to describe in words what he saw around him. His mother called him "Reckless Skald" as much for his tendency to take chances as his skill with words.

Even thinking of his nickname made him blush with embarrassment and pride. Yes, he longed to go a-viking like his father. But just as strongly he longed to be a skald, or bard, like his grandfather Lars Farseeker. Lars had died when Finn was a little boy, but Finn could still picture the lanky silver-haired man, tall and thin as a winter tree. He had sky-blue eyes that glinted as if he had just told a joke. On many nights before the fire, Lars told the tales of Viking heroics. But it was not only the stories that his grandfather had given Finn. Lars had given him a pair of ice skates—his first—that he had carved from a walrus tusk. Finn had long outgrown them, but he kept them hanging from a peg above his sleeping bench.

He stood at the cliff edge and tipped his face to the sky. He closed his eyes, stood still as a stone for a minute, and then recited to a passing cloud:

Wandering on the wave road,
Wondering whence the wind will blow.
Fare thee well my father;
Let the billows bring you back with my brothers
To the hearth of home.

He turned to go. When he reached the path through the rocks that led to the sheep meadow, he stopped. One last look, he thought.

A rattle of rocks behind him made him turn around.

"Finn! What're you doing?"

It was his friend Bo Bluetooth.

"Nothing," said Finn, looking back at the water. "Just watching the sheep."

Wiry and nearly white-blond, Bo scrambled down the slope beside Finn. Finn and Bo ranged around the cliffs and snowfields together, and even shared meals: Bo's parents had been lost at sea on a voyage when he was little, and he lived with his uncle. But his uncle was an old widower, and many times Finn's mother asked Bo to stay for dinner and to sleep over. Bo would help Finn with his chores, but the minute they were done (and sometimes before), they were off to explore the fjords and crevasses, the waterfalls and skerries, stalking eagles and seals, sometimes even spying on the honey-haired Freydis Fairbrow. Freydis had gone adventuring with them just a year before, and she was as adept at stone-throwing and spear-flinging as the boys were. But now Finn found it difficult to speak when she was around. Something about her made his cheeks burn. He became clumsy and dull-witted. Spying on her as she went about her chores with her mother had taken on a special fascination for him.

"Seen them yet?" said Bo.

"Nope. I was just heading back."

"Oh, well. Doesn't seem as if we'll ever see them."

Finn glanced at him, but he was used to Bo, who usually spoke before thinking.

Bo stooped and plucked up a pebble-sized dried

sheep turd. He flung it at a tall outcropping at the edge of the cliff. It hit dead-on, then dropped into the sea.

The wind from the sea lifted Finn's hair. He laughed and stooped to pick up a dried turd, too. But something caught his eye out on the water. He straightened up and blinked. His breath caught and his heart raced.

He squinted and shielded his eyes with his hand. Far, far out on the horizon, there was a small shape that could be nothing but a sail.

a ship arrives

"**M**other!" cried Finn as he charged into the yard, Bo right behind him. The chickens and the goats scattered. "Father has returned! I've seen his sail!" Even their old dog Rollo managed a hoarse bark. Then he whimpered as if he'd hurt his ears.

His mother was tending the cabbage patch on the sunny side of the stone shed where the animals were sheltered at night. When Finn bounded into the yard, she straightened up and dropped her hoe. "What did you say?"

Finn grabbed her by the hands and tugged. "I've seen his sail," he shouted again. His mother looked at him with a distant expression. In her blue eyes rose the rolling swells of the sea, the swells that swept across the ocean tracts to foreign shores. The breeze ruffled her long gold hair and she brushed a strand aside with the back of her hand. Now she focused on Finn standing before her.

"Are . . . you . . . sure . . . ?" she said as Finn led her out of the garden. She touched her free hand to her hair and patted it as if to make sure every strand was in place.

"Look," said Finn, pointing out to sea.

Beyond, in the inlet sheltered by the outer skerries, a wand of sunlight reached through the clouds to light the square sail of the arriving ship. The vessel moved swiftly across the glittering water.

His mother shielded her eyes. "I can't quite make it out. But it could be ..."

They looked at each other.

"Let's go!" shouted Finn. He pulled his mother's hand and they broke into a run, Bo staying close behind them. They scattered the chickens and the goats again as they raced past the farmhouse and took the path down the hill. Rollo gave another try at a bark. It came out sounding like a squeaky creak. He whimpered as they disappeared down the path.

Far below, they could see the ship angling across the inlet, slicing through the blue-green water with a sharp white wake. The ship seemed to be coming on faster.

"Careful now," panted his mother. "Oh, not so fast. It's too steep!" She laughed and glanced at the sea again as they bounded past outcroppings of rock glinting in the sunshine and cut across the slopes of thick grass shifting in the breeze like an animal's coat. They raced into the settlement, passed the low stone church and the few houses and sheds and pens, and ran to the beach.

Already the other villagers had gathered there—only twenty people, for the settlements in Greenland were small and the people liked to live apart from each other. Each villager had a loved one aboard *Dragonwing,* a father, a son, a brother, an uncle, a nephew. The waves splashed ashore with the sound of applause. As Finn got to the water's edge, he turned to see Freydis trotting down the path to the beach.

Finn's great-uncle Floki Falconeye, an old Viking who no longer went to sea but who served as the settlement's lookout, climbed to the top of a jutting boulder at the end of the beach.

"Whose ship is that?" gasped Finn's mother. "Is that Olaf's ship? How sharp are those eyes of yours, Floki?"

Finn's heart hammered in his chest. Oh, his father had returned! Now he would sail, now he would sing to the sun and the stars and the sea, now he would be a man! He danced a circle around his mother. She smiled at him. Then she looked back toward the ship, blinked into the sunlight, and squinted.

"Mother, dance with me!"

She shook her head.

"No, Finn, I've waited too long. There are some moments you cannot dance away."

"What do you see now, Floki?" called one of the villagers. "Is it Olaf Farseeker?"

"Could be," he said, shielding his grizzled brow with his hand. "Must've changed sails, though. He set out with a red sail with a black dragon on it. This one has red and blue diamonds."

Finn strained his eyes toward the ship. It was moving fast but not fast enough to satisfy him. He stared so long that his eyes burned.

One of the villagers grumbled, "Come on, come on! Hurry up, Vikings! What ship is that?"

At last he could make out the curved swan-neck of the prow. Yes, the ship appeared to be the size and shape of *Dragonwing*, the ship he knew so well, the ship that had been one of his playgrounds when he was little: eighty feet long by eighteen wide, stout enough to carry cargo but swift enough to make long ocean crossings.

Then figures aboard the ship came into view. The silhouette standing by the tiller—that must be his father. He squinted, trying to make out his father's trim fox-red beard with the gray sprinkled in it like ashes. He could almost hear his gravelly, bellowing voice.

Hurry, ship, he thought. Race home across the dolphin road.

"Yes, I can see it now. Different-looking rig altogether," said Floki. "Maybe they had to fit out different after a storm."

Finn looked at his mother. She was no longer smiling.

Now she raised her hand against the sun. She looked out at the ship with that expression he had seen so many times before while his father was at sea: a faint smile on her lips, but tears in her eyes.

"That's not Olaf I see waving from the bow," said Floki. "No, that's not *Dragonwing* at all."

Standing on the beach, Finn felt the sun that had risen within him sink into the cold sea of his heart. He looked again, turned away, looked again. For once, Bo said nothing. He saw Freydis glance in his direction. What Floki said was true: This ship slipping toward them was not *Dragonwing*. He looked down at the small waves slipping onto the beach. A dark poem came to him.

Wind, you made a fool of us,
You made us hope.
Now winter has come again;
Is that your laughter
I hear, or just the waves
On the beach?

He took his mother's hand and together they watched the ship come to shore.

"Why, that's Leif Ericsson," said Floki as he climbed down from his perch. "Yes, that's *Sea Sword*, Leif the Lucky's boat."

STOWAWAY

A log shifted in the bonfire, sending a shower of sparks into the pale night sky. The water lay still as ice in the thin blue light. This was the time of light, when the sun never sank too far below the horizon. Even at night, the world seemed no darker than dusk. *Sea Sword* lay at the far end of the cove, her bow on the sand, the rest of her hull in the still water. Her snake-necked prow made a silhouette of a sleeping sea dragon. On the beach, the villagers joined the twenty Vikings from *Sea Sword* around the roaring and crackling fire to listen to Leif the Lucky.

"Yes, we are headed to the land across the western sea," he said, "even though it is growing late in the season of voyages. Many days will pass before we see our homes in Brattahlid and the calm waters of Ericsfjord again." He hoisted a horn of beer and drank. Then he wiped his mouth with his sleeve. "Bjarni Herjolfsson gave me sailing directions. You might have heard the tale of how he and his crew were blown off course on their way from Iceland to Greenland. When they finally saw land again, it wasn't Greenland, that they knew: It was a rich and fertile land of thick forests and meadows. Others have ventured there, too, or so I've heard, but Bjarni's directions are the most detailed. There is a cove there, he told me, in a sheltered bay that is surrounded by white sand beaches. It would make a perfect anchorage. He says that the land is covered with timber and sweet grass for fodder. The fox and the mink are everywhere. The deer and the bear. The partridge and the duck. We'll bring home timber and furs. We could use another ship to help on this voyage of discovery and exploration. Where is Olaf Farseeker?"

Finn's mother stepped into the firelight.

"I am Helvi, Olaf's wife," she said. "Olaf and my two older sons, along with the other crewmen, sailed for the same land last season. They, too, got sailing directions from Bjarni Herjolfsson when he put in here the season before they left."

The fire crackled and spat. The smoke rose and swayed in the faint breeze.

Leif smiled at her. "Then we shall sail after them and join together when we land. Take heart, Helvi. Leif the Lucky and Olaf Farseeker will return with tales of great adventure and treasures to prove them. We sail tonight.

Now, I want to be sure that the directions Bjarni gave Olaf square with the ones he gave me. Helvi, do you remember them well?"

"I do," she said, "and what I can't tell you, Floki Falconeye can. Finn, you better go check on the flock. We've been down here a long time, and the sheep need to be put in the pen."

Finn wanted to shout, "No!" He wanted to listen to the Vikings discuss the voyage, the same one his father and brothers had taken. It was as close to them as he'd come in ages, and now his mother wanted him to tend to the stupid old sheep.

"But Mother, the sheep are fine, they're in the upper pasture, and . . ."

She silenced him with a sword-sharp glance. He knew he couldn't disobey her, especially not in front of the Vikings and the other villagers.

He turned and went up the path, grinding his teeth in anger. Upward he climbed till he reached the house. He grabbed his spear and went off after the sheep.

But even the sheep wouldn't cooperate. He knew he was too angry to round them up. He stalked up the hillsides after them and spooked them before he could turn them toward home. They skipped away from him and stood just out of reach looking at him with puzzled eyes.

In the grayish twilight, he sat down on a rock and

looked at the bonfire far below on the beach, the dark form of *Sea Sword* in the water just beyond. His anger began to thin as he surveyed the world below. A small breeze had sprung up and brought to him the smell of woodsmoke and roasting meat.

He heard a sheep bleat. Then, just the way a poem coasted into his mind like a gull crossing his field of vision, an idea came to him.

Leif, he knew, was going to the land to the west. His father was already there. It was simple. He must go with Leif. Yes, he must sail across the sea to find his father . . . but how? Leif would never allow him to go along. He already had his crew. If he dared ask his mother, she would forbid it. She needed him to help tend the farm.

There was only one way.

He stood up. He felt as though feathers floated in his stomach. Yes. This was what he had to do.

He sprinted down the hill—slipping, falling once, picking himself up—all the way down the slope to his house. He went inside, panting, and removed the leather satchel he used on hunting trips with his father and brothers from a peg on one of the timbers. He had to hurry. "We sail tonight," Leif had said.

Into the satchel he shoved his fur hat, his thick woolen tunic with the hood, the small knife Floki had given him, his extra pair of soft leather trousers, his fur boots, and the special stone called a sunstone that his father had given him before he left on his voyage.

It had been the night before *Dragonwing* shoved off when the family was sharing their last meal together in front of the fire. His father looked at him, firelight flickering across his red beard. He said, "Finn, now it is time for you to take care of your mother. The farm is hard work, and you must do your best to keep it thriving while we are gone. When we return, you will sail with us when we go a-viking again." He paused, then dug into his pocket. "Until that time, keep this as a reminder of the glorious days to come. Someday, my son, this precious stone will be your eyes. Treasure it."

It was then that his father had laid his hand on Finn's shoulder.

"Do I have your word that you will obey your mother and tend to the farm as if it were yours alone?"

Finn nodded. Inside a voice called out, "But I want to go to sea with you! I want to soar over the waves and go to distant lands and see Skraelings and other wonders!"

"Let me hear you say it, Reckless Skald," said his father, smiling.

"I . . . I promise," said Finn.

His father grinned and clapped him on the shoulder. "Very well, Finn. I know I can rely on you."

But Finn wasn't so sure himself. He thought of the

endless stretch of days tending to the sheep that lay ahead of him. How boring, how pointless, how childish! No, he wanted to break free and sail the open ocean. He felt a glow of anger inside him, but he dared not speak.

Finn kept the sunstone in a small leather pouch. Now he removed it from the pouch and weighed it in the palm of his hand. It was opaque, square, and seemed to emit a greenish, milky glow.

His father had said the sunstone would one day help him see. Finn, feeling the heft of the sunstone in his palm, felt a different weight on his heart. He knew what he was doing to his mother. He knew what he was doing to the promise he'd made to his father. But his father had said the words just the same. He felt the small weight of the sunstone in his hand. That day, thought Finn, will be coming soon now. I am off to seek it.

Then he returned the sunstone to its pouch and shoved it deep into the satchel. He glanced at his toy spear standing in the corner and the small harp that he was learning to play. No, he would leave them behind. This was no time for a child's toys.

That was it. He was ready. As if for good luck, he touched the skates his grandfather Lars had carved for him. He went to the doorway and stopped. He peered back into the house. Here was the shelter where the family spent the long winter days and nights playing chess, eating before the fire, listening to his mother play the harp, telling tales and singing songs and poems. Here was the center of his young life, the sleeping bench where he dreamed his dreams of becoming a famous skald, the haven of warmth and love where all voyages began.

He thought of his mother and how she would talk about his father with a faraway look in her eyes, how she would sometimes climb the headlands with Finn to scan the sea for a sail. He knew his leaving would hurt her—he had to face the truth—and he knew how much she would be left to do alone. There was no doubt that Floki would help her, and the others, too, but there was no denying that his leaving would be a hardship on her.

Leaving, too, would be to break his vow to his father.

But he was, after all, Olaf Farseeker's son. The need to seek far horizons was in his blood. He had grown more impatient every day of these long months of staring at the horizon, waiting for his father's sail to appear. With Leif's arrival, the time had come. *Sea Sword* was more than a ship. She was a messenger, and the message she delivered was, *Sail with me to find your father.*

Surely his father would understand.

He took a deep breath and stepped out into the pale night.

In the yard, Rollo hobbled over to him stiff legged,

like a table walking. He nuzzled Finn and whined. Finn kneeled and scratched the dog behind his ears. "I'll be back, Rollo. I promise. Now you take good care of Mother." Rollo whimpered and licked his hand.

Finn stood up and looked beyond the house to the inlet below and the beached ship, the people gathered around the bonfire before it. He took one more deep breath. He was setting off down the path when he heard footsteps coming up. He ducked behind a boulder.

"Finn?" It was Bo.

"Right here." Finn came out and shouldered his satchel.

"What're you doing?" said Bo.

Rollo wobbled over to Bo and licked his hand.

"I'm sailing with Leif," said Finn. "I'm going to find my father."

Bo's eyes widened.

"Leif asked you to go?"

"Not exactly. I'm going to stow away." At those words he felt his stomach tighten.

Bo grinned. "So you're going on a voyage, a voyage of discovery!"

"Listen, Bo. I have an idea. Why don't we go together?"

Bo's mouth opened. Light seemed to flash in his eyes. He began to smile. But then the smile faded.

"Finn, I can't. I just can't. My uncle . . ." He looked away and shook his head.

There was a silence. The sounds of the waves splashing on the beach below reached them. Finn thought of his mother.

"I know what you mean," he said. "But I've got to go."

"How're you going to get aboard without anyone seeing you?"

Finn looked down at the beach. The bonfire was far enough away from where the ship was anchored, but there was still a good chance that someone might spot him moving across the beach.

He looked back at Bo.

"I've got an idea. Let's go."

Before he headed down the path, he scratched Rollo behind the ears.

"Good-bye, old boy," he said. "Take care of Mother."

CHAPTER 4

Face-to-face
with Leif the Lucky

The cry of "more beer" went up from the sailors down by the bonfire. Finn hid behind a boulder and waited to catch his breath. He could see Bo's silhouette moving into position on the rocks above the bonfire and the people gathered there. Only if someone were staring into the gloom might he be seen crossing the beach. He would want only one person to see him: Freydis. But she was nowhere to be seen.

He swallowed hard. The weight of his satchel pressed down on his shoulder. Still, he would have to run as swiftly as he could.

He waited until the distant sound of Leif's men chanting a song of the exploits to come reached him. He could make out "Down the whale road, down the whale road, down the whale road, we'll go a-viking." He waited. Now was a good time, he thought. What is Bo waiting for?

Then he saw it: Bo began hurling dried sheep turds at the people as fast as he could. He rained the dried missiles down on everyone. Finn heard cries of "Hey! Stop that!" and "What's going on here?" and "Is it hailing?" It was the diversion he needed. Then he took a deep breath, crouched low, and moved as fast as he could across the beach. The dragon-necked prow towered above him. He waded through the water by the hull and climbed up to peer over the rail. No one had seen him run to the ship and no one seemed to be aboard. He swung his leg over the rail and landed on the deck. Then someone cleared his throat. He froze. He heard someone sniff—a huge, wet sniff. He looked into the hold. A cow and three goats stood chewing hay. On the rail by the tiller three ravens were tethered to a perch. One went "cronk, cronk" when he eased himself into the hold and crawled beneath the deck where the bales of hay and straw were stored. He fashioned himself a cave beneath the bales and made a pillow of his satchel. Now all he had to do was wait. What would they do when they found him? How long would it take them to discover him? Would they be at sea by then?

He listened to the tiny waves breaking. The noise died down. Bo must have run for the hills. The villagers would figure that Finn and Bo had been up to their usual mischief. After a few minutes, he heard shreds of laughter coming from the beach.

He was comfortable, if cramped, in his nest. The rich smell of hay and animals and manure filled his nostrils.

But he was not calm. He began to wonder why he had decided to stow away, why he was hidden among goats, a cow, and ravens to be taken away from his mother and his home, Bo and Freydis. What had he really done? He pictured his mother coming home, thinking that Finn was tucked in bed after his exploits with Bo, only to realize that he was not there. But he did, at times, sleep in the upper pastures with the sheep. So maybe she wouldn't find out that he was missing till the morning. What then? He imagined how she would feel—the new pang of breathless sorrow in her heart, the tears welling in her eyes. A fat drop broke loose and skated down her cheek. She looked around, calling for him. Rollo hobbled out to lick her hand. Even the old dog emitted a gravelly whine. Then his thoughts leaped to the future—a future empty of him, lost over the horizon. He pictured a mammoth wave looming up to swallow *Sea Sword*. He sank into the endless depths beneath the blue-green sea. And there stood his mother on the bluff, a small breeze riffling the grass beside her, looking out to sea with tear-blurred eyes.

Maybe this isn't such a great idea after all, he thought. Maybe I should just go home and wait to see if my father and brothers come home. They might be just about to appear over the horizon, and be home in time to cook their breakfast over the bonfire.

He started as a deep voice called, "Give me a leg up!"

and the men began to thump and bump and clump aboard. He felt the ship rock as the men began moving about. There was burping and banging and cursing and laughing. He heard the squeak of blocks as the sail was raised and the clunk of wood on wood as the crew manned the oars. There were shouts of "Farewell!" and distant calls of "Good luck!" and "Godspeed!" from ashore.

Blood thudded in his head. It was too late! There was nothing he could do. He could not jump up now and run to Leif, saying, "Put me ashore, I don't know how I got on your ship, but I can't go, my mother will be angry, and the sheep are probably dropping off the cliffs into the sea, so let me go!"

Mother! he thought, tears banking up in his eyes. I'm sorry!

He squeezed his eyes shut and gulped a breath of air.

No, he could not bolt now. He thought he would be seen as a fool—a childish fool. He had made his decision. He took another deep breath. No, he would have to go on.

He felt the ship begin an easy rocking over the low waves. Soon the crew had rowed the ship across the inlet to the skerries and the open water beyond.

Finn heard Leif call out, "Ship your oars and slack the sheets!"

After more bumping and thumping and clumping, he felt *Sea Sword* heel and bend and slither through the seas. It seemed to him that the ship felt much freer and happier with the wind in her sail.

He wished he could feel freer and happier. Now he felt trapped and miserable. What had he done?

The ship rocked through the swells. The lines creaked and the hull groaned. Another sound came to Finn's ears, a strange guttural sound. Maybe one of the men had brought along a wild boar, and it was snorting just above him on the deck. He listened, and at last he realized that the sound was one of the sailors snoring. He almost chuckled.

Even though he was tense, Finn began to feel drowsy. The easy rocking of the ship and the song of the lines and the hull slipping through the water added to his drowsiness. He didn't want to fall asleep. He wanted to stay vigilant, to be ready for whatever was going to happen. How long would it take for someone to find him? He could lie here for days, maybe a week. Maybe the ship would have to turn back. Maybe a storm would hit them and they'd have to return to the village and he could slip off the ship and nobody would know what he'd done.

Now even his nervousness wore him into sleepiness. His mind was racing but his eyelids drooped. As he was falling asleep he wondered if his mother knew he was missing. He thought of the pastures overlooking the ocean. He might never see them again.

A stinging pain in his ear woke him and he cried out, "Ow!" He sat up and hit his head on the deck above him. He turned to see a black-and-gray puppy inches from his face. This time the puppy licked him. But then it started barking short yips—it wanted to play. Finn tried to grab him. He heard footsteps above.

He grabbed the puppy and pulled it close to him. The pup sank its teeth into Finn's sleeve and began growling. He waited, his heart thundering. Footsteps—slow, heavy, deliberate—came closer. Then they stopped.

Finn held his breath.

He heard someone step down onto the deck with the animals.

He heard a nasally voice say, "Who's in there?"

He saw a bale of hay get pushed aside.

The puppy bit him hard in the hand but he did not make a sound. Another bale was pulled aside and now he saw a figure peer in at him. He was a gaunt man with long black hair and blue eyes that did not look in the same direction at once. He made a growling sound deep in his throat and reached in to grab at Finn's leg. Finn pan- icked—but he could not move. He felt the thin piercing stab of the man's clawlike fingers on his ankle. The puppy squirmed out of Finn's grasp, launched himself at the man, and sank his teeth into his hand. The man pulled his hand away and bellowed an oath. The puppy scrambled back to Finn.

From up on deck, Finn heard another voice say, "What's going on down there, Kormak?"

He could see the man rubbing his hand. "I found a stowaway, that's what's going on down here."

Finn heard a heavy thump on the deck and a gigantic figure pushed Kormak aside to loom above him. With the puppy held to his chest, there he was, face-to-face with Leif the Lucky.

going a-viking

F inn saw Leif's great hand reach toward him, grab his tunic, and drag him from his hiding place. He clutched the puppy to him.

Leif held him against the sky. He thrashed and kicked to free himself.

"Well, what have we here?" said Leif. The crew gathered around and peered down at them. "Two puppies? Look, Sven. Your puppy has a puppy of its own."

The men laughed. The puppy barked. A round, red-faced man with a curly beard ambled over, smiling. "Little Wulf has found a big brother," he said.

Leif laughed. "Are you a little fish that's looking for its mama?"

The men laughed again. Finn stopped struggling and the puppy stopped barking. With Finn in his grip, Leif stepped up onto the deck.

"Are you a rat from the bilge? Or are you just a common, everyday stowaway?"

The crew began to laugh again, but Finn blurted out,

"I am Finn the Reckless Skald, son of Olaf Farseeker. I am sailing with you to find my father and brothers in the land across the sea."

Leif cocked his head and raised an eyebrow. Leif's arm never quavered in spite of holding Finn and the pup up in the air. Slowly he lowered Finn and then set him with a thump to the deck. "My, my, but we're in the presence of a skald," he chuckled. "And at what court do you declaim your verse, Finn the Reckless Skald? None? What do we do with skalds, men?"

The men looked at each other.

"Do we throw them overboard?"

The men looked at each other again.

"Do we tie them to the mast?"

Finn saw a young man push his way past the crewmen. He didn't look much older than Finn himself. He was short and stocky and had flyaway hair the color of red fox fur. He said with a Scots burr, "Aye, we do much worse to them than that, don't we, skipper?"

"That's right, Red. If we decide to keep them aboard, we make them work."

The men were grinning again—except for one of them. Kormak frowned at him.

"This is not a good omen, Leif," he said, an ominous tone in his voice. He rubbed his hand as he glanced at Finn. "Stowaways bring ill luck."

Leif frowned. "Kormak Ravenkeeper, when I want your opinion, I'll ask for it. This is no ordinary stowaway. This is Olaf Farseeker's son, and a great skald to boot. We should consider his presence a sign of good fortune."

Kormak Ravenkeeper shot Finn a dark look. "I'll be keeping my eye on you," he said.

"As far as you can," said Leif, sparking a few chuckles among the crew. Kormak stared at Leif, began to open his mouth to say something but stopped himself, then pushed through the crew to stand by himself at the stern.

"Where was I?" Leif said. "Ah, yes. We make stow-aways stand lookout, coil line, haul the sail, cook, and, most of all, take care of the animals. Sven, I don't mean you."

He looked at Finn as if making a decision. He looked at the sky, then out to the horizon, forward, and aft. Behind them, small icebergs and skerries were scattered in the distance. The cliffs hung low on the horizon. Ahead lay open water.

"We can't take you home, Finn the Reckless Skald. The wind's with us now and so's the current, and they'll be against us if we return. We're off on a venture, and there's no turning back. It seems you'll have to go a-viking with us."

Now it was Finn's turn to smile.

"Why, thank you, sir."

Leif held up his hand. "You won't be thanking me once you get a taste of the real Viking life. Isn't that right, Red?"

Red glanced at Leif and then slowly nodded.

"And you won't be thanking me," continued Leif, "when your father hears that you ran away from home and left your mother to tend to everything herself."

Leif turned and rested his hands on the rail. He stared out at the rolling blue waves.

"It'll be a long and dangerous voyage, Finn. Only a few have made the crossing to the western lands, your father among them, it seems. Your job is to care for the livestock and help the sailors. Sven will be your master, but Red will show you the work of a Viking."

Red looked at Finn and grinned.

"And," Leif said, looking around with a twinkling smile, "you are also to give us a poem when I ask for one."

"I would be honored," said Finn. He glanced toward the stern. Kormak Ravenkeeper was true to his word. He was watching Finn. He did not look pleased with what he saw.

a good sign

The sun climbed high in the sky as *Sea Sword* sliced through the waves. Finn noticed that the water had gone from a greenish blue to dark blue. First the skerries had dropped from view behind them, then the last tips of the highest sea cliffs. At last they were in the open ocean.

"Follow me," said Red. "We've got chores to do." Finn's duty was to throw a bucket with a line overboard and haul up seawater to slosh onto the deck. He tossed the bucket into the water and it filled up so fast it almost pulled him overboard. Red helped him haul it up.

"It'll get the better of ye if ye don't watch out," said Red, grinning. "Now try it again, and just skim it."

"Thanks," said Finn.

"Ye'll get the hang of it," said Red as he mopped the planks.

After they finished with the deck, they tended to the animals. Finn took a pitchfork and mucked out the old straw, tossing it overboard. Then he spread new straw and gave the animals their food and fresh water from a cask.

When he and Red had finished with the animals, Leif called for Finn. "It's time you took a watch," he said.

Finn scrambled to the afterdeck, Wulf galloping after him.

He took the tiller and squinted up at the sail. The breeze blew fresh and warm, the sky looked clean and washed, and the waves rolled and sparkled. Many times his father had let him steer *Dragonwing*. Finn even had his own small boat to paddle in the bay and coves and out to the skerries. On the skerries he and Bo would fish and explore, watching the whales and seals and flocks of seabirds.

Sea Sword swung easily under his touch. He loved the way the ship seemed to be alive, the way it seemed to swim through the waves. It had a different feel from *Dragonwing*, a tighter, harder action when he moved the tiller, but even more flexible when it climbed a swell. Finn quickly grew accustomed to the helm. It made his heart sing, and a poem began to form itself in his mind.

"It seems we have a sailor in our midst," said Leif to Sven. "But I thought he was a skald as well, yet we've heard not a syllable of verse pass his lips. What about it, Finn?"

Finn had never recited one of his poems to anyone but his mother and father—not, of course, unless you counted the seabirds, the fish, his dog Rollo, the sheep, and the wind. Forget his brothers; they made fun of him most of the time, so he chose to sing to the creatures whose silence he could always regard as approval.

But he knew that he had boasted that he was a poet. Now he had to prove it.

"All right," he said, swallowing hard. "I have one I've been thinking about since I came aboard. But you should know that...that...I've...I've never sung one of my poems to anyone, apart from my family, before."

"Then we shall be honored with having known you at the dawn of your fame," said Leif with an exaggerated dip of the head.

Finn cleared his throat. "Well, then," he said. "Here goes."

Swift as a seabird,
Daring as a dolphin,
Sea Sword the sure-footed
You race across the rearing waves
To bring the brave ones
On a journey made for giants;
Sail on to the setting sun
And carry us back to Greenland in glory.

When he was done, Leif and Sven glanced at each

other. Leif said, "Maybe your boast is not hollow. Maybe you are a singer of the sea." One of the ravens croaked a call.

Kormak Ravenkeeper laughed. "Don't be fools. You call that a poem? My ravens make more poetry than this young whelp." He laughed again, glaring at Finn all the while with his wide-spaced gaze. "Quit while you're young, boy, and keep bailing the bilge. You excel at that."

Leif said, "Kormak, you've a mighty harsh tongue these days. Is something bothering you? Is the salt cod not to your taste? Have you not gained your sea legs yet?"

Just then *Sea Sword* rose high on a swell.

"Look!" cried Sven. "Dolphins!" Four dolphins veered toward the ship and swam beside the hull as if to challenge *Sea Sword* to a race. Finn watched them dive and spin and crisscross in front of the bow.

Sven laughed and clapped his hands. "It's a good sign," he said. "Yes, no matter what Kormak says, it's a good sign for the voyage."

dirty weather

Finn crawled into the nest where he had stowed away. This was to be his berth on the voyage. He let Wulf snuggle down beside him. He was so tired that he fell asleep instantly, but he woke himself up snoring. The ship rocked onward. He wanted to fall back asleep, but now he began to wonder, once again, if he'd made a mistake. He was already far from home. Red and Leif and Sven were friendly enough, but they were strangers. He felt a cold trickle of fear at the thought that he would not be able to make it. Maybe he would lose his ability to steer well, to do his chores, even to come up with poems at Leif's command. And then there was Kormak, who always seemed to be standing somewhere just behind him, watching him, as if he were waiting for him to do something wrong.

He lay on his back, listening to the lines creak and the water gurgle by the hull beneath him, and he thought of his mother, her face lit by firelight, and she was smiling at him.

I'm far from home, he thought. I don't know anyone. I want to be home. I wish Father had never left.

Wulf rolled over and whimpered in his sleep. Finn laid his hand on the puppy's warm belly.

I should never have come, thought Finn just before he fell asleep.

In minutes, it seemed, Red was telling him to get up. He crawled out of the straw and went on deck. The sun was already high. He rubbed his eyes.

"There's our young stowaway," said Leif. "Have you got your sea legs yet?"

Finn nodded.

"Then it's your turn to be the lookout," said Leif. "Up there." He pointed to the masthead and smiled.

Finn had always liked climbing the mast of *Dragonwing* when he was helping his father take care of the ship. His job was to shimmy up to the top to apply pitch to the wood to keep the rot away.

Without saying a word, he began climbing. Halfway up he realized that the doubts of the night before had vanished. Maybe it was even the few hours of sleep that had helped. Maybe it was the effort of climbing the swaying mast. Whatever it was, he was glad to reach the masthead and survey the great reach of ocean around him. Up here, he felt as if he were flying. The wind ruffled his hair and the ship rode the waves beneath him. The waves themselves stretched away in an unbroken procession as far as he could see. The sun sparkled on the blue water.

As the days unfolded, the more comfortable Finn felt aboard *Sea Sword*. His loneliness began to lessen. He listened to the groan and creak of the rigging as the sail pulled it taut, then eased as the ship worked her way over the backs of the waves. He ran his eyes over the bell shape of the sail, a crescent like the sliver of moon that rode above them in the pale night skies. He lay on his back at the bow and looked up into the blue. He sniffed the sharp salt smell of the sea and eyed the blues, greens, and grays of the water. At night, he watched the wake of *Sea Sword* glow green and glitter like the moon's path. He took note of the flight of the gulls and petrels and gannets and fulmars, all the birds that Leif studied to calculate his course. He climbed the rigging to the top of the mast and looked over the ocean to see the thin line of the horizon, the endless waves and once, in the distance, icebergs to the north, a pod of whales to the east, and walruses to the west.

Sometimes, rocking at the masthead, he would squint at the waves and imagine that the rumpled back of the sea was the serrated spine of a sea dragon slithering toward the ship. This was the open ocean, the realm of sea monsters, if the tales were true. He blinked again and the dragon's back would turn to whitecaps. He wondered if anyone else felt this fear, this fear mingled with excitement, but he dared not speak of it.

But not everything on the voyage agreed with him. His routine of standing watch, keeping lookout, and tending to his chores left little time for sleep. He was always tired, and found that even the plain, hard planks of the deck were comfortable enough for a nap if he had a spare moment. Meals were only dried or salted salmon or codfish, hard bread, dried apples or cherries, and beer or milk, since making a fire for cooking endangered the ship.

The care and feeding of the animals was a chore he liked no more aboard ship than he had at home. The ripe tang of the cow manure made him think of the responsibilities he had left to his mother. Even a milk cow and two goats hobbled so they couldn't ramble around the decks were a nuisance to Finn. He viewed the time it took to muck out, feed, and water them as time stolen from what he loved the most—steering the ship and watching the waves.

Only the ravens were off-limits to him. Kormak would not let him tend to them. But every time Kormak was on watch, Red sneaked them bits of food. One night when Kormak was at the helm, Finn went with Red to give the birds some dried fish. The birds seemed pleased with the treat, clacking their bills and puffing up their feathers and preening.

"Why is Kormak such a sour old eel?" asked Finn when they had returned to the hold.

"He treats everyone like bilge," said Red.

"You'd think he would be happy," said Finn, "being the master of the mighty ravens and knowing their secrets."

"Sven says it's because of what happened on a trading voyage long ago. There was a thick of fog, and the ship drifted for days. Kormak let his ravens fly to find land. Well, they found it. His ravens led the ship onto a reef, and all hands drowned. Except for Kormak. The skipper and some of the crew were Leif's cousins. Kormak and his ravens made it to a skerry, and they were rescued by other Vikings. No one ever forgot that it was the ravenkeeper who survived, the one who had led the ship to the rocks. Some blame him to this day."

One night, when he was watching the moon, Finn realized that a ring had grown around it. It was a ring as colorful and mysterious as the flowing curtains of the northern lights.

"What is that?" he asked Sven. Sven was steering the ship and Finn was teaching Wulf to sit. He pointed up at the ring of light that glowed around the moon.

"That's a sign, Finn," said Sven. "It means we're in for some rough weather." Just then the ship staggered over the top of a big wave. "And it's coming soon."

Leif joined them at the helm and gazed at the ring in the sky.

"Yes, I've felt a change in the seas," he said. "Tell the men to secure everything and get some rest. We may be in for some dirty weather."

Finn went to the bow to feel the ship ride the rolling swell. He felt the immense force of the water through the hull as it surged higher with each passing wave. He gripped onto the rail and peered into the dimness to see a high pyramidal wave passing beyond the ship. Moonlight glinted on its cap.

"You could be riding that wave."

Fear flashed through Finn at the sound of the words. He spun around to see Kormak standing inches behind him.

Kormak placed a bony hand on Finn's shoulder. "Yes, it would be so easy, boy," he continued in his harsh whisper. "A simple helpful shove and you'd be riding those waves you admire so much."

Finn knocked Kormak's hand away.

"Get away from me," he said.

Kormak snorted.

"Very well," he said. "But take my advice: Watch yourself."

For a long time, as Finn lay below, he could not quiet his heart. The image of Kormak standing behind him—

and the sensation of the bony, birdlike clasp of his hand on his shoulder—made him shiver. He knew Kormak could have pushed him overboard. He knew he would have to take his advice and watch out. He felt frightened—frightened at being alone, frightened at having made an enemy for no other reason than being himself.

All night long, Finn lay awake. He felt the seas building. No longer did they rock *Sea Sword*. They began to shove the ship this way, then that. He could see them growing. They would surge by, darkened monsters sweeping by with malice on their minds.

By morning, black shredded clouds raced low over the water, rain slashed down, and the wind blew hard and cold. The waves thundered past them like black mountains with white foaming glaciers pouring from their faces.

At first the Viking spirit stirred everyone, Leif included, and they steered *Sea Sword* before the blow like a runaway sleigh. Over the crashing swells she surged, down into the troughs she plunged, up again into the foaming whitecaps she charged, the Vikings hollering over the wind in exultation.

But the wind blew harder, and soon *Sea Sword* threatened to sail out of control.

"Ease off there on the lines!" bellowed Leif over the roar of the wind and the hissing and rumbling of the waves. "Reef the sail now!"

Kormak, streaming with the pouring rain and sloshing seawater, stumbled aft to relieve Leif at the helm.

He said nothing, but he cocked a black eyebrow and fixed Leif with one eye as if to say, "I told you so, but you wouldn't listen."

He cast a look at Finn. Finn looked away.

The wind blew harder still. Soon Leif's command was "Drop the sail!"

But the sail would not drop.

Leif squinted up at the masthead. "I need a volunteer," he yelled. "That sail needs to come down now or we'll open a seam."

As if he were watching someone else, Finn saw himself step forward and say, "I'll go."

Leif twisted around to look at him, but before he could speak, Finn scrambled for the mast and began climbing. The ship lunged into a wall of green water and seemed to stand still for a moment. Finn was almost wrenched away from the mast. His legs flew outward and he kicked as he gripped onto the slick wood. Then the ship shuddered and shook off the sea and lunged forward again, the sail whipping Finn's face as he made his way upward. The rain felt like pebbles clattering against him.

The higher he went, the more the mast lashed back and forth. The sail flogged him. His fear grew as he twisted around for a look: Below him were the faces of the men turned up to look at him, *Sea Sword* looking slender amid the froth of the seas extending out to disappear in the rain and gloom.

He looked up. Against the streaking black clouds he spotted the thick line of the halyard at the masthead. It had jumped the pulley in the block. He grasped the flailing halyard and shook it, but the line was wedged. He'd have to shimmy to the very top to free it.

Now he could feel his entire body shaking from fear and fatigue. His hands quivered. I cannot hold on any longer, he thought. But in the next instant he fought upward, feeling that with each moment he would be tossed into the sea, flicked off the mast by a giant unseen finger.

At the top he draped his arm over the yard of the sail. Everything was in motion: the mast waved back and forth, the yard dipped and swayed, the clouds hurtled past, the sail cracked and thundered, the ship leaped and lunged. But he managed to grip the line just below the block. He gave a mighty heave and jerked the line free. In the next moment the yard dropped away from beneath him and he tumbled after it with a small scream. That moment froze in his mind: He knew he was headed downward to be dashed to the deck or flung into the sea. He saw the Vikings looking up at him, the spume-streaked seas on either side of the decks. And he felt himself become feathery as he fell.

But just as quickly the yard stopped and he smacked against it and gripped on with all his strength. Then the yard and sail worked their way slowly downward, controlled now by the Vikings handling the halyard below.

Hands gripped him and pulled him off the yard when he'd reached the deck. The men furled the sail and lashed down the yard.

"I can see you're living up to your name, Reckless Skald," called Leif as he struggled with the steering oar. He was not smiling. A wave loomed behind him, lifted the stern, and tossed a gush of water onto the deck. "Next time, wait for me to give you the order to go aloft."

Sven helped Leif lash the tiller to the rail and everyone hunkered down beneath the canopy. They would run before the storm with a bare mast, the only way to weather such a blow. The cow mooed, the goats bleated, and the ravens, brought under the canopy, shook their wet, puffed-out, and windblown feathers and looked irked.

Finn clutched Wulf to him and watched waves as big as cliffs roll past. He still shook from his climb, but he also felt his heart thrilling with excitement. The sensation of being flung to and fro as he clung to the mast had been exhilarating—even if he had been within a fingernail of flying off into the tumult of the sea.

Sea Sword dived and swerved, bounded and plunged,

climbed and dived, driven over the waves by the rising wind. "There, there," he said to the puppy. "Everything will be all right." He realized now that sea monsters weren't what he had to fear. It was the sea itself. Wulf whimpered and licked him on the chin.

He turned to see a giant green-black sea lunge over the rail. He just managed to gulp a breath of air before the icy water pounded down on him. He felt himself becoming lighter, more buoyant. First there had been the roar and screech of the wind. Then the world quieted. He clutched Wulf and felt himself rising. He was going over-board!

Into his ears came the rush of water closing over him. The light became greenish and dim. Time began to slow down. He felt weightless. He tipped his head to look down: There was nothing but green gradually turning black below his feet. Then a lighter form began to take shape from below. Quickly it rose toward him. It was a human form and he recognized it. It was his grandfather Lars, swimming toward him as swift as a salmon. Had he entered the realm of the Viking dead, where the vanished ones lived on?

He was beginning to black out from holding his breath when he felt a painful tug on his leg. He was spun around and the water washed away and he could hear again. The water sizzled in his ears. The wind beat down on him. He banged against the ship's rail. A powerful grip seized his shoulder.

He landed gasping on the deck, water sloshing around him. Wulf pulled free from Finn's encircling arms and coughed up seawater. He shook, spraying salt water from his fur.

Above him, Red stood gasping, every bit as wet as Finn himself. The ship lurched into a breaking sea, spray shooting into the air to be slapped and flung away by the wind.

"Not a good time to be going for a swim," he panted, gripping onto a line and spitting seawater. Then he grinned. "Lucky Skald might be a better name for ye. Next time, the ocean might decide to keep ye. And I might not be there to fish ye out."

black fog

A barrel of beer had been washed overboard, but the goats, the cow, the ravens, Wulf, and the men emerged safe, if wet. They ate a quick breakfast of dried salmon and stale rye bread, then set to bailing out. Wulf paddled around in the sloshing seawater as if it were a pond.

By the next morning the seas and wind began to calm. Leif said, "How far off course the storm blew us, I'm not sure."

"Should we send the ravens?" said Sven.

Finn knew from his father that some sailors used ravens to show them the way to land. His father was the only one he knew who used a sunstone to find his position. Very few Vikings came to possess a proper sunstone. His father had traded three polar bear skins for the precious piece of calcite on a trip to the Faeroes.

"We'll have to wait," said Leif. "I think we're too far from shore. Look at the color of the water." They looked down at the dark blue water.

"Did we get blown to the north?" asked Sven.

Leif checked the overcast sky.

"It seems that we're far to the south."

To Finn, it seemed that they were lost.

He hesitated to tell Leif about his sunstone. The captain was the ruler of the ship. Leif might take offense if Finn offered it to him. He might view it as questioning his seamanship.

The wind quit and a black fog rolled across the water to swallow them. In a day the swells calmed and the sea became a plain of liquid iron. But no one could see beyond the rail for the fog. The ship creaked when the men moved about the deck. The sail hung slack. Moisture from the fog beaded up on the lines, on the men's beards, and on the fibers of their woolen tunics. The world went silent and gray. Everyone spoke in whispers. One of the crewmen said, "Maybe we should have brought a priest along, to help us pray."

"Pray all you'd like, if you're the praying kind," said Leif. "We need all the help we can get."

In thick, muffling fog, they drifted for two more days. Leif said to Finn, "Look at the water." Finn peered overboard. Even though the ship seemed to be standing still, Finn could see dimples and ripples in the water by the hull.

"A current is taking us somewhere," said Leif. "But where it's taking us is anyone's guess."

After another day of thick fog, a brief breeze chased the fog away, but still a heavy overcast covered the sky. Leif told Kormak to send the ravens flying. Kormak mumbled, "At last, we'll find our course again."

Finn glanced at Red, wondering if he, too, was thinking about the shipwreck of many years ago. Red returned his glance and raised his eyebrows.

Kormak grasped the birds and flung them into the air, calling after them, "Earn your keep!"

All three of them circled once around the ship, croaked a loud call, and settled back on their roost. They made a few quiet croakings and groomed their feathers.

Red snickered and Kormak scowled at him.

Leif shook his head. "If your ravens were half as good at navigating as looking after themselves, we'd be setting a sure course."

Kormak said nothing but stroked the ravens' ruffled feathers.

Finn made up his mind. He dug out his sunstone from his satchel and brought it to Leif.

"What have we here?" said Leif.

"It is a sunstone," said Finn. "My father gave it to me. He said that he uses a sunstone to help him find out where he is on his voyages. He traded for another on one of his voyages, and he gave it to me."

Finn handed the stone to Leif. It was a small square

stone, nearly clear but smoky inside. Leif turned it in his fingers. Sven peered over his shoulder.

"He said it can find the sun for you even when the sun is hiding," said Finn.

"I've heard of these," Leif said, holding it to the sky and squinting at it. "But I've never used one."

"My father has used it many times," said Finn. "He says he would not sail without it."

"If Olaf Farseeker swears by it," said Leif, "it must be worth a try."

"I've heard of men who use a sunstone to find their position," said Sven, "but I've never seen one myself."

"Well, anything's worth a try now, isn't it, Sven?" said Leif. "We've been drifting for days."

He looked at Finn.

"Show us how your father uses it."

Finn took it between his thumb and forefinger and raised it. He squinted at the stone and eased it across the sky. He swept his arm one way, then the other. He searched one section of the sky, then turned around and swept the sky behind him.

"The stone captures the glow of the sun," said Finn, "so you can get a fix to tell where you are. But I don't see anything yet."

He swept his arm across the sky again.

"Floki Falconeye said that it captures the light of the

sun," he said, "as if it was rain in a bowl. Oh! Look at that!"

In the center of the stone a disc of light glowed like a magic eye.

"Bring the bearing dial," shouted Leif. "We'll take a bearing and set our course, boys!"

Finn handed the sunstone to Sven.

"By God, there it is," exclaimed Sven. "Glowing right there where it wasn't before."

Finn watched Leif make his calculations based on the height of the sun and the eight points on the bearing dial. Finn had seen his father use the bearing dial before, too. The points corresponded to the eight named points of the horizon—north, northeast, east, southeast, south, southwest, west, and northwest.

When he was finished, Leif barked at the men to set the sail.

He grinned at Finn.

"If this pebble points us true, I'll owe you when we reach shore."

Sven handed the stone back to Finn. "Take good care of your magic stone," he said. "We may need it again."

"Kormak, maybe you can get those ravens to lay eggs," Leif said. "They're not much good for anything else."

One of the ravens croaked at Leif.

Finn thought of the days when he wished for a way to see beyond the horizon. Now, in a sense, the sunstone had given him that power.

He went below. He nestled the sunstone into its pouch and stowed it deep into his satchel.

CHAPTER 9

RED'S STORY

Finn felt his leg being shaken as though it were a length of wet rope. He cracked open one eye to see Kormak sneering at him in the dull twilight. Kormak let go and Finn's foot thudded to the deck.

"Your watch, poetboy," he growled. "Time to roust your carcass and get to the tiller. Now get moving. I need my sleep."

Finn groaned and stretched and rolled to his knees. The boat slid down the face of a wave and he tumbled and bumped against a wooden rib.

The fog had cleared and a wind had risen. But this wind appeared to blow from every direction. The waves, too, seemed to leap and burst from everywhere. *Sea Sword* wallowed through them, lurching one way, bucking another, the sail taut in the wind one moment and slapping loose and sloppy against the mast the next. Men lost their balance, tripped over each other, and bickered among themselves. Gray rumpled cloud covered the sky.

Finn staggered onto the deck, a new feeling rising inside him. It was not a pleasant feeling. It felt as though a smaller ocean had formed inside his stomach and sloshed around every time the ship rose and fell with the jostling seas. He made it to the rail by the tiller. Red was already steering, his grin aglow in the pale light.

"Looks like we've got this watch together," he said. "Hey, ye don't look so great."

"I'm all right," said Finn, staring out at the constantly moving water. "I'm just a little tired."

"Well, ye look green to me," said Red. "This is the kind of fluky sea that can make even the toughest Viking seasick."

At the word "seasick," Finn felt the ocean inside his stomach rise. The dried fish he ate morning, noon, and night seemed to swim inside him. His mouth became watery. He definitely was not feeling well. He clenched his mouth shut and concentrated on the horizon.

"Aye, it can happen to the best of us," said Red, pulling the tiller toward him and glancing up at the sail. "Why, I've been so sick myself that all I could do was lie on the deck curled up like a fresh fallen lamb. Ye can get so bad ye'd wish for someone to come give ye a blow over the head with a broadaxe, just to put ye out of your misery."

Finn looked back at him.

"Please, Red. Stop talking about it."

"I'll tell ye one wee story about it. I was coming home with my father one day after three days out hauling our nets in the Sound of Sleat. The weather had been blowing stink the whole time, and then it turned fluky on us and blew the way she's blowing now, coming from every known direction."

Finn felt a cold sweat begin to ooze out of his clammy skin. He wished he could lie down on the cold wooden deck. He tried to turn his thoughts to something soothing. He thought of his dog Rollo, but the memory of his damp fur, smelly as rotting seaweed, came to mind. Then he thought of his mother, and at first the image of her warm smile and soft voice made him feel better. But then he saw her stirring a pot of fish heads and cabbage, the food they'd had to eat one year when the hunting and fishing and farming had not produced well, and his stomach creaked.

"I was cold, wet, tired," Red continued, "and the only food we'd had was a piece of old raw mackerel. My father never liked to eat the catch since it meant sacrifice later on."

He stopped and laughed. "Ye never knew what the old man would come out with next. A fighter he was, a fighter even to the day the Vikings came and took his sheep away."

His voice grew softer. "That's how I came to go a-viking. I was swept up with the livestock and carried away to Greenland. That was five years ago, during the time of voyages. My old man lay chopped down by a Viking sword, his claymore still gripped in his fists. My mother and sisters I haven't seen since. The Vikings who took me bartered me for one of Leif's goats. He's always treated me fairly."

Finn looked at him. For a moment his churning stomach made no difference, and he thought about Red as a little boy running away in fear from the Viking raiders. How the sight of his father being cut down must have been burned into him! How could he have grown to forgive his father's killers, to work among them, to be one of them himself?

"Never mind about the past," said Red. He laughed and shook his head. "I'm a Viking now, thanks to Leif, and past is past. I could no more go home to work the waters and the pastures of our wee isle than I could become a raven and fly at Kormak's command."

Finn's stomach groaned.

"But to tell ye my story: The wind turned sour on us and we beat about in the tiny boat for another two days. We could not make headway up the loch to home. My gorge rose higher and higher, till I felt my mouth get wet. I clamped my jaws shut to keep my stomach down. I willed myself not to let myself fall to seasickness, but...."

Finn had closed his eyes. He felt weak. He gripped the rail and thought that the only thing that could save him was a big wave that would wash him overboard and pull him into the cold, deep sea.

"...but in the end my stomach rose up like a swell and the sweat jumped out on my forehead and I flung myself to the rail and out flew the chunks of mackerel I'd eaten not long before. I kept at it till my stomach was dry as an empty fish barrel and even then I couldn't keep my head from hanging over the side, nothing coming from my mouth but my stomach trying just the same. My father clapped me on the back and told me what I just told you. 'Happens to the best of us, Red my lad.'"

He looked back at Finn. His smile grew brighter. Finn was gripping onto the rail, his head draped overboard, his body convulsed in paroxysms of nausea. He understood every word of Red's story. All he wanted was a wave to tilt the ship enough to dump him into the water to end his misery.

Red laughed. "What did I tell ye, Finn? It can happen to the best of us. Just ride with it. I'll keep us on course while you lose your stomach."

CHAPTER 10

Bjarni's directions

Sea Sword sailed on over the blue-green sea. The sky held a pale light even at night, but Finn noticed that the light was weakening as the days marched toward autumn. The men told tales of former voyages as the days of sailing wore on. They trimmed the sail and tended to the animals. The breeze held and the sailing was fair. The crewmen, when they weren't on watch steering the ship, took turns sleeping or doing chores. Many times Finn had to step over a Viking slumbering in the shifting sunshine as he went about his duties.

Finn got used to the routine of doing chores, keeping lookout, steering, eating, and then sleeping for what always seemed like a few short minutes. Now even a few stars glittered where before only a dim dusk covered the sky. One evening, after his watch, Finn went to his nest in the straw. The ship clipped across the seas, heeling at a comfortable angle, cresting a wave, and then slipping into the trough. He lay on his back and called for Wulf, who curled up beside him. He heard the sounds of the animals, the cow with her deep breathing and the goats with their chewing and clacking teeth. Warmth radiated from them along with their sour-milk smell.

Most of the men didn't want to sleep with the animals because the space was too cramped and they wanted to be on deck so they could be at the ready in case of danger. Sometimes Red would burrow down in the straw, but all that would ever escape his mouth was "'Gae night, Finn" before he began snoring in counterpoint to the sounds of the animals.

Finn lay with his fingers laced behind his head, Wulf a furry warmth beside him. Beyond the overhang of the deck, he could see the pale stars swaying across the sky with the movement of the ship.

Should I find Father, he thought, just how angry would he be that I have disobeyed him? And Mother—I don't dare even think about Mother. I have disobeyed my father and betrayed my mother. The others better be helping her. And the stupid sheep better not have wandered off or been snatched by eagles. And Rollo—I wonder how Rollo would get along with Wulf?

Perhaps I should not have come on this voyage, he thought. I'm so far from home. The bottomless sea lies inches from my back. I may never see my mother again. Will I get seasick again?

He squeezed his eyes closed. Fragments of ideas for poems and other notions flitted through his mind. *The moon courses through clouds like shreds of spirits... The sunstone sees what captains can't... Waves toss their manes and race the wind... Schools of clouds... Pods of clouds... Leif's eyes that seem always slanted in a smile... My father's gravel-throated laugh... My mother's way of making up nicknames, like mine, and calling Einar "Funny Fox" because of his reddish hair and his jokes... Does anyone miss me... I hope Rollo is healthy... Wonder what Bo's doing... Does Freydis miss me?*

He opened his eyes and sighed. What's done is done, he thought. I must not falter. I have become a man. There's no going back. I steer the ship. I do the chores. I keep lookout. I sing my songs of the sea.

He lay his hand on Wulf's side and stroked the sleek fur. The puppy whimpered and wriggled closer.

No, thought Finn as he drifted toward the entryway of sleep. No, I must not falter.

Three days later, the water turned blue-green again, and flights of puffins appeared. Leif said, "If Bjarni's directions are correct, I'd expect that we'll soon sight the rugged land of glaciers that he mentioned."

That afternoon the lookout cried, "Land ahead! Land

ahead!" The entire crew rushed forward and peered into the distance. Sven stayed at the tiller.

No one moved as *Sea Sword* rolled toward the land, each man riveting his eyes on the distant shore. The men placed bets on what land it would be. "It's land we've never seen before is the only bet I'll place," said one of them.

At last the first sharp teeth of a mountainous barren island came into view. They sailed close enough to it to see that it was covered in rocks and stones and, high in the mountain passes, huge white glaciers.

"Yes, Bjarni was right," said Leif. "This is a barren place. We'll call it Helluland, the land of rock slabs."

Finn could see that no grass or trees grew on the island. He scanned the slabs of rock for human signs—for a sign of his father and brothers. Nothing but rock and mountains met his eye.

"Leif, do you think my father and brothers might be here?"

Leif fixed his eyes on the land.

"Only if they were forced to put ashore. They were headed far to the south. Bjarni said there's a bay with a protected cove there that should make a sound anchorage, the best anchorage along the entire coast. I'm convinced they headed there."

Southward they sailed on favorable winds. Helluland

dropped below the horizon and they sailed out of sight of land for two days. Then, one clear evening, Finn noticed sure signs that they were nearing land once again. The water turned a pale shade of green, yellow weed floated on the waves, and seabirds of all sorts this time—puffins, gulls, dovekies, auks—wheeled above their wake, flew in flocks over the water, or paddled on the waves.

Then up came the cry of "Land!" from the lookout, and a cheer went up from the men.

"Bjarni hasn't steered us wrong yet," said Leif.

Something in Leif's voice made Finn glance at him, and he caught a look of concern on his face. He saw him frowning toward this new land, checking the sky, watching the sail, scowling at the sea. He noticed that Leif's jaw muscle twitched.

They sailed closer to the coast, and saw that it was thick with forests. Leif named this land Markland. The lookout said that the water toward shore looked full of shoals, so they headed off again on a course to the south.

"The land we seek cannot be far," said Leif to Finn as Markland dropped astern. "But I worry that though Bjarni's directions have been good so far, they may yet lead us wrong."

Sven laughed.

"Don't listen to him, Finn," he said. "Leif only starts to worry when things are going well. He's been like that ever since we were boys back on the farm in Brattahlid. He likes it better when the weather's rotten or he's lost. He has more to do."

Finn looked at Leif. Leif was staring at the masthead as if he hadn't heard a word.

In another two days, they neared a long stretch of golden sandy beaches and dunes that Leif named Wonderstrand. For an entire day they sailed past a continuous beach with no sign of an inlet.

"This can't be it," thought Finn. "Bjarni's directions told of a protected bay with a cove perfect for anchoring."

Soon the Wonderstrand disappeared behind them. Once again in the open sea, the men began speaking in lower tones. Finn suspected that they were growing anxious about how long the voyage was taking.

"We'll be there soon," mumbled Leif the next morning. "I'm sure of it."

Finn wondered what would it be like to set foot on a place he'd never seen before. What kind of animals lived there? But there was only one question that he ached to answer: Were his father and his brothers there? Had they built a settlement? Would they be waiting for him?

If they weren't waiting, he knew that Leif would search for them.

All that day *Sea Sword* surged across the rolling seas.

Leif stayed on watch constantly, gripping the tiller till his knuckles turned white.

Finn woke early the next morning to give Wulf a good brushing. "That's a good boy," he said to the pup, who thought that brushing time was playtime. He spun around and grabbed the brush in his jaws and began tugging.

"Give that back!" laughed Finn as Wulf shook his head. "That's no toy, Wulf. Drop it!"

From on deck he heard one of the crewmen say something in a voice so low he could not understand it. Someone answered in an excited tone. Wulf yanked the brush out of Finn's grasp just as he heard "That's it! There it is!" The sound of running feet rumbled above him as he jumped for the deck.

He ran to the bow and wormed his way between the men to see ahead.

There, in the crystalline morning air, lay a low line of land. The men were quiet as they strained to see their destination.

"Is that it?" Finn asked.

Everyone turned to look at Leif.

He nodded.

"If Bjarni's directions are right," he said, looking past the men to the land ahead, "then that's it."

When they sailed closer, they could see dense forest

and rolling hills. Here and there the forest was broken by meadows. A long sandy beach came into view. The beach curved far inland, sweeping around to form a bay.

Leif said, "Everyone keep his eyes on the land. We've got to watch for Olaf and the crew."

"What about the Skraelings, Leif?" said Sven.

Leif shrugged. "They're rumored to be a fierce people. But sometimes rumors turn out to be false. We'll deal with them if we have to. We have armor and broadswords and the hearts of Vikings."

As the ship sailed along the coast, Leif studied the land.

"There's no sign of Skraelings," he said. "But let's round the point to see what lies ahead. Maybe that's where *Dragonwing* is."

They sailed around a long spit of beach with tufts of grasses waving in the breeze under the bright blue sky. Finn looked from one side of the bay to other as *Sea Sword* ghosted ahead. Where was *Dragonwing*?

"See that cove over there?" said Leif, pointing. "That must be it."

Finn could see no ship at anchor or on the beach. If this was the place, the ship was no longer here. He began to wonder if Bjarni's directions were right after all. Or was it that Leif might not have followed them correctly? His father may have sailed to another cove altogether.

"Sven, go forward and guide us in," said Leif. "I want to see how close we can get to shore."

Now Finn could see the thick stands of fir trees and hear the wind sighing through the needles. The sound of waves washing ashore soothed his ears. The scent of grasses and pine pitch and flowers came to him on the breeze. Somewhere in the beach grass a cricket chirped.

"We'll go ashore here," said Leif. "Douse the sail and man the oars."

The crew scrambled to drop and furl the sail and set to rowing. *Sea Sword* glided over the shallows, the sandy bottom of the cove showing clearly through the water, the shadow of the ship rippling over the ridges of the sand.

"You can bring her right to the beach," called Sven from the bow. "It's sandy bottom all the way."

Sea Sword made a soft crunch on the sand as she landed. The men shipped their oars. For the first time in weeks the ship was motionless. A sudden quiet spread over the world. No longer did lines creak or timbers groan. Wavelets lapped at the hull. The firs whispered in the wind.

Finn glanced at Leif. The look of concern was draining from his face.

Leif chuckled.

"How about that, Sven?" he said. "We come all the

way to the other side of the world and sail right into our anchorage. You'd think we're back at Ericsfjord."

Now he strode to the bow, spun on his heels, spread his arms wide, and boomed, "We did it, boys! By God, we did it!" His face beamed with joy and relief. "An extra ration of beer for everyone tonight! A feast of fresh venison! Now, let's go ashore and feel solid ground beneath our feet!"

From the crew burst a round of cheers. They slapped each other on the back and pointed out features on the land they wanted to explore. Finn felt his heart juddering: This was it. This was what he had been waiting for. This was knowing the reality of sailing for weeks across an unknown sea to come ashore on an unknown land. He felt faint with giddiness.

As he watched the men vault overboard to splash onto the beach, his heart began to calm. Yes, this was landing on an unknown shore, but something was missing. He scanned the bay again to be sure he hadn't missed an unseen inlet.

Yes, *Sea Sword* had arrived. They had made a safe passage. But *Dragonwing* was somewhere else.

"Let's go, Wulf," he said, gathering the pup into his arms. He handed the dog down to Sven, then leaped into the shallow water and walked up on the beach. Wulf was already ahead, throwing himself into the sand, rolling, and scampering around in circles, kicking up puffs of sand.

"Looks like someone's glad to be ashore," said Leif, laughing.

Beyond the beach was a meadow covered in wildflowers and grapevines. A wall of dense forest bordered the meadow in the distance.

"It's beautiful land, isn't it?" Leif said as Sven and Finn followed him up the beach. "It'll be a good place to let the animals graze."

"If the Skraelings don't kill us all first," called Kormak from the ship. "I've heard about them. And there are one-legged creatures in these lands that eat men's hearts, too. Danger is everywhere. You won't catch me rushing ashore till we've got our shelters built."

Leif strode on, ignoring the comment.

"Pay no attention to Kormak," he said. "He's still miffed about his cowardly ravens."

They walked along the beach, Wulf bounding behind them, till they reached the other side of the cove. The solid earth beneath Finn's feet after so many days on the rollicking sea seemed to rise and fall and tilt like *Sea Sword*'s deck.

The ship dropped out of sight around a bend in the beach. They trudged onward, scanning the beach and water before them.

"Look at this," said Sven. He walked to the edge of a meadow and bent down. "Wild grapes," he said, cupping a large purple bunch in his palm. "Look at them all. The field's full of them."

"Good for making wine, eh?" said Leif.

The land spread out before them, but there was no sign of Olaf. There was no sign of *Dragonwing*. The beach grass swished in the breeze and a few puffy clouds sailed overhead, casting their shadows on the land and sea below.

"Wait a minute. Over there," Leif said. "It looks like a ring of stones, a fireplace."

They walked over to inspect. It was a fireplace filled with charcoal. Finn surged with excitement. Had this been his father's camp?

Leif squatted and dug his fingers into the ashes. "Stone cold," he said, but then he pointed. "Footprints."

The footprints led off into the woods. "I'm certain those are Skraeling footprints," said Leif. "Now is not the time to follow their trail. Soon, however, we will seek them out to trade with them."

"And search for my father?" said Finn.

Leif stood up. He surveyed the land around them.

"Yes, we will try tomorrow. But we have much to take care of if we are to winter here. We'll need to build our houses, hunt for food. You, Reckless Skald, must be patient. If your father is here, we will find him. Or he'll see smoke from our fires if he's near. Now let's head back."

Finn followed along, his excitement just as quickly replaced by disappointment, as they trudged back through the sand to the ship.

CHAPTER 11

chief

"The Skraelings have been here," said Leif to the crew when they returned. "We found rocks that had surely been a fireplace, the charcoal of a fire, footprints. They seemed to have moved off long ago. My guess is that Olaf Farseeker and his crew are living somewhere in this land. Perhaps they put in somewhere near here, and tomorrow we'll have a look for them. And we'll also get started building our houses. Inland there is good timber. We saw signs of deer, mink, and fisher. But this land belongs to the wild grape. It's growing everywhere, on the hillsides and meadows, more grapes for wine than I've ever seen. We'll call this place Wineland, boys, a land of wine for Viking voyagers."

Finn wondered why they didn't start searching for his father and brothers that day, but he held his tongue. He must try to be patient.

But he spent the night in his nest aboard *Sea Sword* burning with anticipation. His father might be just beyond the cove or through the woods. There were so many places to look.

Lying awake, the image of the forest of Wineland came to him again, and the shadowy figure stepped out from the trees as usual to refresh himself with a handful of water.

At sunrise, Leif, Sven, Finn, and two crewmen set off down the beach. The others who remained behind were to work on *Sea Sword,* to make repairs, clean the hull, and mend the halyards and sheets that had frayed during the voyage.

They soon found that the woods were so thick with vegetation and deadfall that they could make little progress through it. They spooked deer and partridge from the thickets, but they found no human sign.

That evening they returned to the cove, crosshatched with scratches from brambles and branches and pocked with mosquito bites.

"We'll need to concentrate on getting settled," said Leif as he sat down with a sigh on the beach. "Everyone needs to help. Fall is coming soon, and when the leaves fall, exploring this land will be easier."

"And searching for my father?" said Finn.

Leif glanced at Finn. "Yes, Patient Skald," he said. "We'll search for your father. I'll have scouting parties go out to look for the Skraelings—and your father—but we'll not mount a long search until we've got the houses built and our camp secure."

The next day, the Vikings set to building their settlement. Some of the men began to fell trees and haul rocks and cut turf to make their houses in a clearing above the beach. Some were detailed to catch codfish, herring, and salmon and prepare them for drying on wooden racks they built on the beach. Finn worked alongside them, paying close attention to Sven and staying out of Kormak's way. Red worked with him, too.

Throughout the day, Finn would pause to scour the land and the sea for any sign of his father. I've come all the way to Wineland, thought Finn, just to do exactly what I was doing back in Greenland.

Everyone returned to the ship to sleep that night. Finn crawled into his nest with Wulf. He reached into his satchel to get his heavy tunic. The night was clear and chilly.

He pulled the tunic out and put it on. He was about to tie up the satchel and make a pillow of it when he realized that he hadn't seen the sunstone pouch.

He dug his hand in and fished around for it. Then he pulled the other items out. He held it up and shook it. He pawed through his clothes. He turned the satchel inside out.

The sunstone was gone.

He knew he couldn't have lost it. He never took it out of the satchel. But he began to doubt himself. Could it have worked its way out of the satchel somehow? He patted the straw all around where he slept. Wulf cocked his head and tilted an ear as if to ask, "Is this a new game?"

But Finn was in no mood for games.

There was only one answer. One of Leif's men was a thief.

His first impulse was to go tell Leif. But what good would that do? Leif might think that Finn had been careless and had simply lost the sunstone.

But it was no good. He kept returning to the reality of the situation. Someone had taken it.

He thought he would tell Red. But what if Red himself had stolen it?

No, Red wouldn't have taken it.

He lay down in the straw and tried to sleep. But he kept puzzling over the sunstone. He could not imagine where it could have gone, unless someone had helped it disappear. Leif himself might ask him for it again, and then what would he say? "Oh, sorry, Leif, I seem to have misplaced it."

Then a name came to him: Kormak.

If anyone had a reason to steal it, it was Kormak.

His ravens had failed. He seemed to hate Finn. And Leif had made him the butt of a joke.

No one else would have a reason to take it. He wanted to take his anger out on Finn. He must have known how much the sunstone meant to him.

The question was how to get it back.

By dawn the next day the crew was back at work. Finn helped haul logs from where they fell to where the men were setting them together for the house. Three, four, five trees were felled, and Red and Finn took axes to the limbs. The air resonated with the scent of pine pitch.

As he worked, Finn continued to watch for his father across the water, on the skyline of a hillside, in the thick stands of fir trees—and now he kept an eye on Kormak. Had he really stolen the sunstone? Maybe the best way to get it back was to walk right up to him and demand it back. But Kormak had no reason to give it back. Finn pictured Kormak giving him a nasty grin and saying, "So now the young skald is making false accusations. What kind of a stowaway do you have on your hands, Leif?"

In the afternoon, Finn helped dig the foundation. He used a pick to chop through the turf. He helped roll boulders aside and build a rock wall. He was sweating hard in the warm sun.

The sweat did not wash away thoughts of his father.

During a break he saw Kormak talking to one of his

ravens off by the woods. When Kormak looked over, Finn looked away. He could have sworn Kormak had given him a threatening look.

Over the next three days, the house took shape. Finn kept the secret of the lost sunstone to himself. He decided that he had to bide his time. He couldn't confront Kormak—not just yet.

But what he couldn't understand was why Leif did not search for Olaf. When the house was finished, would they go searching then, as Leif had promised?

Wulf played as Finn worked, and after the work was done Finn worked with Wulf. He taught the pup to sit, heel, stay, and come. By now, Wulf was growing from a fluffy black and brown and gray ball into a muscular young dog with sharp ears and a nose for game. He was learning his lessons well.

On the evening the first house was finished, Sven and Finn were down at the smooth beach where Finn took Wulf to train him. The sun settled into the slick silvery sea, lighting the sky above it pink and pearl.

Sven said, "Finn, I have watched you with Wulf. You have listened well to my lessons. I brought him aboard to be a work dog for me, but I can see that he has become more attached to you than to me."

The sun sank out of sight below the horizon. A few gulls flapped slowly across the glowing sky.

"A boy needs a dog," he said. "Wulf is yours."

Finn kneeled before Wulf and rubbed him behind the ears. "Do you hear that, boy?"

He looked at Sven. "Are you sure?"

Sven nodded and swatted at a mosquito.

Finn looked into Wulf's chestnut eyes and wondered why he felt a sinking feeling inside to still be called a boy. Surely now, after a voyage across the sea to an unsettled land, he would be considered a man. But no.

He looked into Wulf's eyes and felt tears welling up inside his own. He thought of his mother and Rollo and the view from the farm out to sea.

I'm in the middle of nowhere, he thought. I was stupid to stow away and leave everything and everybody behind. We're not even searching for my father.

The thought of the sunstone came to him. Now was his chance to tell someone. Sven was honest. He might understand. But he didn't know how to say it. When he ran the words through his mind's ear, they sounded childish. "I think someone stole my sunstone." Somehow it sounded even worse, as if he were complaining. He should be able to take care of a simple object like a sunstone.

"Let's get back before we get eaten alive by the mosquitoes," said Sven, already walking up the beach.

the keel in the cove

"All right," thought Finn as he lay awake on his sleeping bench. The tang of fresh pine pitch from the just-felled logs filled his nostrils. "If Leif won't go looking for my father, I will."

The sky was a sapphire glow above the sea where the sun would rise as Finn and Wulf left the house. Stars still speckled the sky. The Viking standing watch outside said, "You two are up early," as they passed.

"Wulf needed to go out," said Finn. "I'm taking him down to the beach."

When they got to the water's edge, Finn turned in the direction of the fireplace stones they'd spotted the day they landed. He and Wulf began to trot along the firm, wet sand, and soon *Sea Sword* and the buildings had disappeared behind them.

A fresh-faced day had begun by the time Finn came to the stones. He approached them and kneeled down to finger the charcoal. The footprints had been erased by wind and rain.

Onward they trotted, following the beach that curved away toward a low headland where the beach ended. The sun had risen and stood bright in the sky as they reached the headland. They climbed through the woods and sat down on the top of the rise. The beach began again below them and swept in a crescent along another protected cove.

"I don't care if Leif is angry when we get back," Finn said to Wulf. Panting, Wulf looked at him and tilted his head. "I came here to find Father," said Finn. "Building houses won't find him."

He stood up and shielded his eyes with both hands as he looked at the beach and the cove below.

"Let's get moving, Wulf," he said, taking a step forward. But then he stopped. At the far end of the beach, in the glistening shallows, something caught his eye.

"What is that?" he said, squinting out at the water.

He blinked. There was something in the water, just breaking the surface.

From this distance, it looked like the ribs of an immense whale.

"Let's go take a look," he said, and slid down the incline to the beach. He trotted along the shelving sand, staying close to the water where the surface was harder, Wulf panting along behind him. By the time they reached the spot, Finn could see what looked like the tops of posts or short tree trunks sticking out of the water.

As he waded out to them, he realized what they were.

"The keel and ribs of a ship," he whispered to Wulf. He pushed out into the knee-deep water and ran his hands along the ribs. Yes, the keel and ribs looked familiar to him. He had been only five years old when his father and brothers built *Dragonwing*, but Finn knew how to tell if this was it. He splashed to the bow and the broken stem. As he peered below the surface of the water, he felt his heartbeat trill.

Yes, there they were, just barely apparent beneath a coating of black slime and barnacles. Carved deep into the wooden stem were three sets of initials: GF, EF, FF. His brothers had helped him gouge his mark as the ship's keel was being laid. He reached into the water and dug his fingers into the indentations to clear them of the growth.

He straightened up and looked around him. A gull flapped across the empty sky. The breeze awoke and shifted in the beach grass. Only the sound of the small waves came to his ears.

"Let's go," he said to Wulf, and he splashed to shore.

The sun was still making its morning ascent when Finn returned with Leif and Sven. A breeze had come up and made a hushing sound in the grass behind them.

"It's *Dragonwing*," said Finn in a voice almost as soft as the wind as they reached the wreck.

The tide had gone out farther. They waded out to the wreck in ankle-deep water.

"Sure looks like a Greenlander's ship to me," said Sven, running his hands along the wood. "Oak keel, pine deck... what's left of it, that is."

"It's *Dragonwing*," said Finn. "That I'm sure of."

Finn showed them the carved initials.

Leif ran his fingers over them and then walked around the wreck, examining the ribs and keel.

"By the condition of the timbers, the wreck's been here over a year." He scowled at the line of trees just beyond the beach. "They must still be here somewhere. If they made it ashore at all. This ship is in rough condition. It looks like it's been stripped of anything that could be carried easily."

Finn squinted at Leif. In a quiet voice, he said, "Are you going to search for them now?"

Leif looked hard at Finn.

"Boy, you make everything sound simple," he said. "We're as likely to get lost looking for Olaf as we are to find them. You saw for yourself how thick these forests are. We must be patient. Our plan is to stay the winter, so the time will come when searching in this unknown land makes sense. Besides, if they're anywhere nearby, they'll see our smoke. And they would have heard us building our camp."

"So you never really planned to search, did you?" said Finn, surprised at the anger in his voice. "They could be right over that dune and we'd never know. This wreck was here but if I didn't come looking we'd never have found it."

Finn saw Leif's eyes flash.

"Careful, Reckless Skald. Remember that you were a stowaway that I could have tossed to the waves instead of carrying across the sea. And don't you go wandering away by yourself again. I'll lock you up with the goats if you do."

He turned and splashed through the water to the beach.

Finn looked away. He felt a sting in his eyes as he touched the roughness of a rib. He stared at the three submerged initials.

"We'd better get back," said Sven. He began walking back to the beach. Then he stopped and turned. "Are you coming?"

Finn wanted to run in the other direction. He'd found the wreck of *Dragonwing* and all Leif the Lucky wanted to do was go back to his house.

He could not admit to himself that Leif might be right: The forest was so dense that men standing just beyond arm's reach could not be seen. The searchers could become disoriented and wander for days—or longer—with camp only a short distance away.

"You might as well calm yourself down," said Sven. "Leif answers only to himself. If I know him, he'll be searching for Olaf before you know it. He'll just do it when he's ready."

harps and heroes

The golden grass alive with the autumn chorus of crickets soon was covered with the first snow. The crew finished sheds for the animals and for the gear. The first ice appeared on the ponds, though the cove stayed ice-free. The maples shed their orange and yellow and red leaves. Great Vs of geese ribboned southward. In the night sky Finn saw the dazzling stars in the shape of the warrior rise higher as the temperature sank lower day by day. Sometimes the warrior loosed a star like a sudden spear that would streak across the sky. Finn and Red skated on the new ice with skates they'd made from a buck's antlers. The fires in the houses burned at every hour.

But what Sven had said about Leif still hadn't come true. Leif and a small band of men made a few treks away from camp to "spy out the land," as Leif said, but he made no mention of going to search for Olaf in the farther reaches of Wineland. Finn had not been part of these brief expeditions, remaining behind with Red and the others to help with chores.

One windy night when the wolves and the wind howled outside, everyone gathered as usual in the main house. The light from the crackling birchwood fire fluttered on the walls and the smoke from the fire gave the room a misty look.

They had finished eating their feast of venison, partridge, and corn gruel. Some of the men were playing chess. Others watched. A few dozed or held quiet conversations.

Finn watched and listened as Sven, strumming a small harp, accompanied one of the men playing a flute carved out of a sheep's leg bone.

On many nights Sven played this small harp, and Finn thought he had heard such a beautiful dreamlike sound only once before, and that was when his own father strummed the harp and sang the songs of the ancient heroes.

Finn yearned for the harp that he had to leave behind. Luckily, Sven had let him play his harp. He had even taught him a few new tunes.

Every evening after dinner, Leif called for music and song. Always he asked Finn to recite a story or poem. Finn told of the voyage, or about something that had happened during the day's work and exploration. Sometimes he made up a story or a poem, such as one about an imaginary conversation among the three ravens.

"Tonight, young skald," said Leif to Finn, "give us a poem passed down to you from your elders. Your inventions amuse us, but we must also remember the songs passed down to us to keep our past alive. Do you have a favorite?"

"Yes," said Finn. "This is a song my father sang during feasts. He always played the harp along with it."

"Then use mine," said Sven, handing him the instrument.

Finn took the harp and sat down beside the fire.

"This is a song about the great Erik Bloodtooth and his battle against the Scots," he said as he strummed the taut strings of the harp. He glanced at Red, feeling suddenly sheepish. After all, Red was a Scot, and he didn't want to hurt his feelings.

"With apologies to Red," he said.

Red laughed and made a dismissive wave. "No offense taken," he said. "I'm as much a Viking now as a Scot."

Finn nodded and began.

Swordmetal struck
On shining shield,
Men round him moaned
Who fell on that field;

The blink of the blade
The flash of the shafts
All ringed the King,
His axe bright with blood.
His heart beat with bravery
And he spurred on his spearmen
Till they turned the Scots' scourge
To valorous Viking victory.

When Finn struck the last chord, cheers and applause erupted.

When the ruckus died down, Kormak grumbled, "An amateur performance at best."

Leif ignored him. He stood up and took a log from the woodpile. "Remembering the deeds of the past is part of becoming a man," he said. "You've sung us a proud song."

He looked at Sven with a cocked eyebrow and a small smile. "But your harp playing . . . what do you say, Sven? Lacks polish, don't you think?" He tossed the log on the fire and sparks sprayed upward. He brushed his hands together and grinned.

Sven clapped Finn on the back. "Don't worry, boy. It's a matter of practice. Keep it up and you'll be harping with the best of them."

Outside, the wind howled. Wolves, closer now,

howled with the wind. When he saw Leif and Sven glance at each other, Finn felt uneasy. Was it really the wolves that were howling to each other?

"Leif," he said. "When are we going to search for my father and brothers again? You said that once we got settled, we'd go."

Sven and Leif glanced at each other again.

"Soon," said Leif, and turned to the woodpile for another length of wood to add to the fire.

Finn wanted to ask what "soon" meant. He'd heard no more talk about searching. But the wolves howled again, and he did not speak.

The Bluff

Whatever "soon" meant, it wasn't soon enough for Finn.

He lay awake that night imagining what had happened to his father and brothers as he had every night since they'd landed. Maybe they were captives and spent their days being guarded by Skraelings. Maybe they had built another ship and they were sailing homeward, laden with riches.

Or maybe . . . Finn did not want to imagine the other maybe.

He did know that he needed to go after them. Why had he come to Wineland in the first place? It wasn't just to do chores. If Leif thought it was too dangerous to go out looking for them again—and that's what Finn took Leif's "soon" to mean—then Finn himself would have to do the searching. A person traveling solo could thread his way through the forest more easily without the burden of a search party. He knew that Leif's main reason for coming to Wineland wasn't to rescue his father. It was to find new resources. They'd found grapes, grass, timber, and fish in abundance. But even these would require more ships and more Vikings to make use of them all. He would be cautious. He didn't want to put his men at risk before he could return with more ships.

Finn thought of his mother back home in Greenland. He hadn't broken his vow to his father—and abandoned his mother—only to come all this way to let fear stop him. But even the thought of his mother made his stomach crawl with guilt. He pictured her expression when she'd seen *Sea Sword*—not *Dragonwing*—landing on the day that now seemed so long ago, the look of sadness and then of resignation, and he felt a pang that he wanted to banish from himself.

The next morning was cold, overcast, and calm. He fed Wulf, ate his own breakfast, and did his morning chores of feeding the animals and gathering firewood. Then, as casually as he could, he told Red that he was going partridge hunting and that he'd be back later.

He strode off into the woods, his heart trembling. He was at last seeking out his father and brothers. He could not stand the waiting any longer. He had been bursting to do something, and now, finally, he was on his way.

How I miss Bo, he thought. How Bo would love to be heading off into the unknown!

At first he had to push his way through thickets and crawl beneath dense stands of spruce. The trees knit together into a canopy that closed off the sky above him. But soon the thickest forest gave way to more open woodland, and once again the sky appeared.

Leif should have tried going in this direction, he thought.

A gap opened in the shelf of gray cloud to the east. The rising sun beamed through and lit the last orange and yellow leaves of a maple in a brilliant glow as Finn moved past. He marveled at the sight of the glowing tree against the dark gray sky.

He walked until the sun was as high overhead as it would get during the late autumn day. Walking through the dense thickets and stands of spruce and pine was far different from the treks Finn took on the barren bluffs and mountainsides back home in Greenland. There, every moment he was tending to the flock or on a hike with Bo, he could turn to see the vivid sea and the skerries toward the horizon beyond or hunching cliffs and bluffs towering into the sky before him. Here, every tree, every bush, every hill, every swamp, every gully seemed to hide a mystery. He felt light and fluttery, as if he were a bird weaving its way through the corridors of light and shadow. He felt this way because this was what he had dreamed of: to be adventuring on a mysterious shore, to be questing for his father and brothers, to be a man who could strike out on his own. As he followed a vague path through the woods, he knew that this was why he had risked stowing away. The shimmering light filtering through the needles, the blue sky above, the last splashes of red and orange and yellow in the thickets of maples and birch, the quiet only occasionally broken by a distant bird call, the sense of anticipation spurred by the unknown that lay ahead . . . this was why he had come to this place.

Finn peered around him. Patches of blue sky appeared above the spires of the spruces. The sunlight filtered through the needles and made them glisten with the colors of the rainbow. Even though it had warmed up as the sun climbed higher, remnants of the early snow lay in the shadows beneath the trees. A raven cronked, a gull cried, a little bird with a black cap went *"chick-a-dee-dee-dee."*

The afternoon shadows lay long across the forest floor when he reached a high bluff. At the edge was a clearing, and beyond him the woods rolled to the sea. At the foot of the bluff lay a small half-frozen pond. He decided to go down to it for a drink of water.

He slid and slipped down the bluff face, hanging onto tree trunks and boughs as he made his way to the edge of the pond. He stepped onto the slender beach of rock and gravel and squatted before the glassy surface. He cupped his hands and dipped them in, then snatched them back.

The pond water was so cold his hands ached. He rubbed them on his tunic, hesitated, and then scooped up a drink of the icy water.

He was sipping from his hands, the water draining between his fingers and making small splashes on the pond surface, when he looked up to see a figure standing on the opposite bank. The figure's reflection, its perfect double, held still on the water.

The pond was only fifty yards across. Finn froze. He could see the figure clearly, standing as it was in a patch of sunshine. The figure was tall and dark-haired, lean, and, from what he could see, a young man almost his same age. Then the figure bent down, squatting as Finn himself was, to scoop water for a drink.

The name that leaped to mind so surprised Finn that he stood up.

"Gunnar," he said to himself, knowing at the same instant that it could not be Gunnar. "That's Gunnar, and I've found him."

Just as the figure straightened up and began to turn, Finn raised his hand and waved.

The figure stopped at Finn's gesture. He waited, watching. Then, with birdlike quickness, he raised his arm in greeting, turned, and stepped back behind the curtain of woods.

Finn was left breathless, staring across the water, the

image of his brother sharp in his mind. But it could not have been his brother. It was a Skraeling. His first impulse was to run around the perimeter of the pond to chase him down. He wanted to see him up close to be sure he was a Skraeling and not his brother.

But he glanced at the sun. It was easing down through the deep blue of the sky, and he knew how risky it would be to be caught in the woods at night.

He glanced again across the water. The breeze ruffled the surface, and the lowering sun glinted off the ice at the far end. Maybe everything he'd heard about Skraelings wasn't true after all, he thought. Maybe they were not so unlike the Vikings. Why else would he feel such a soaring feeling at such an unmistakable sign of greeting, out here so far from home? If they were so wild and vicious, why would one of them wave in greeting? If they were so different, how could he mistake one of them for his very own brother?

As he turned to go, he realized that this was not the first time he had seen these woods, this pond, the shadowy human figure by the pond. This had been his vision of Wineland, when all he'd known of this land was the descriptions he'd heard around the fire. This had been his vision, and now he was *living* it.

CHAPTER 15

captured

"Yes, I saw a Skraeling," said Finn, pausing as he chewed another mouthful of partridge meat. Firelight flickered over him and the men who had gathered around to hear of his adventure. He waved the drumstick. "And the funny thing about it was that I thought it was my brother Gunnar at first."

A few of the men chuckled. One of them said, "Did he hop on one leg?" and winked at Kormak. Kormak scowled.

"It was half a day's walk from here," said Finn. "I can take you there tomorrow. I found an easier way than the one we tried before." He bit into the meat, tore off a chunk, and began chewing.

Leif sat with his hands clasped together. One thumb was stroking the knuckle of the other hand. He seemed lost in thought, though he listened as Finn spun his tale about the day. Finn glanced at him. He had never seen him so quiet.

At last he spoke.

"So you've proved that we're not alone in this land," he said. "But you've done it by going against my orders."

Finn stopped chewing.

"Orders?" he said, his voice muffled with food. "I didn't know you issued orders about not going to hunt for my father and brothers." He swallowed and set the drumstick down. Again he felt the first hot stirrings of anger.

"Ah, that's where you prove something about yourself, Reckless Skald. You are young still, and sometimes hear only what you want to hear."

Finn felt his ears go red. He started to speak, but Leif held up his hand.

"Let me explain. Since we've arrived, you've been itching to go find them. I understand that. If my own father or brothers were missing, I would want to go find them. But have I not been clear that the time is not right to go searching into the unknown for people who may be anywhere? Have I not told you that I would put you in the goat shed if you were to wander off again?"

Finn felt the eyes of the other Vikings on him. He did not want to look at Leif. He let his gaze drift to the fire. In his cheeks he felt the heat of embarrassment.

"When the time is right," said Leif, "you will be the first to know. In the meantime, I don't know whether to praise you for having the guts to go out there alone—and for being the first to lay eyes on a Skraeling—or to spank you like a little boy for disobeying me. Maybe a night with the goats would make you think more clearly."

Finn could think of nothing to say. He stared into the middle distance, wishing all this would go away.

Leif stood up. "I'll let it pass this time," he said. "But only because it's so late and I wouldn't want you waking up the goats." Then he laughed. "Don't look so glum, Finn. Do you think I would punish our Reckless Skald for living up to his name? No, I will not punish you, but I order you to stay within shouting distance of the camp until I decide we will search for your father and seek out Skraelings to trade with them. Is that clear?"

Finn nodded, but he was nodding to the thought that had just flitted through his mind: that he had to go out again to be sure that the Skraeling he had seen was a Skraeling and not Gunnar, and if it had been a Skraeling, to find a way to ask him if he had heard of three Vikings who had landed here not long ago.

"Good, then," said Leif. "Let's get some rest. We've all got plenty to do tomorrow."

The weather broke blue and balmy the next morning. Finn and Red finished their breakfast of gruel and dried salmon and wandered down to the water's edge in the warming air. Sven had gone out hunting early with Wulf.

"Leif doesn't want to risk sending anyone into the woods," said Finn, "but he doesn't know what it feels like to see someone out in the wilderness who might be your brother. And even if it isn't Gunnar, the Skraelings might know where my father and brothers are."

He stooped to pick up a stone and skimmed it across the slick face of the cove. It skipped away like a frightened frog.

"I'm heading back there no matter what Leif says," he said.

"What do ye mean?" said Red, picking up his own stone.

Red watched Finn's stone skitter across the water.

Finn laughed. "It's pretty clear, isn't it? Go back out where I was yesterday. Find the Skraelings. What else do you think?"

Red glanced at Finn. "But what about our chores?"

"Sometimes chores have to wait," said Finn. "They'll always be there when you come back. Look, there's no time to waste. If you want to come, follow me."

At that he sprinted off down the beach. Red looked toward the house in the distance where the men moved about doing their chores. Then he took a deep breath and scrambled after Finn. They didn't stop running until they'd rounded the bend of the beach and plunged into the woods.

Panting, Red said, "Where're we going?"

"This way," said Finn, ducking under a branch.

"What're we looking for?" asked Red.

Finn stopped and put his finger to his lips.

"From now on, whisper. We're looking for any signs, rocks for a fire, footprints, anything." He turned and headed through the light and shadow of the woods.

Red trailed close behind.

"But how do ye know we'll find any?" he whispered. "What about Leif? He'll kill us if he finds out."

Finn looked over his shoulder.

"That may be," he said. "But it's killing me not going out to look for them." He turned and pushed aside a bough as he walked on. He was surprised that Red seemed so hesitant. Bo would have been leading the way.

They traveled through the woods for a time until Finn came to a clearing and kneeled down. Red kneeled beside him.

"See that bluff up ahead?" said Finn, catching his breath. "That's the one I climbed. I had a view of woods stretching to the coast lying far, far away. The pond was below. I went down to it to get a drink of water. That's when I kneeled down, and when I glanced up, I saw the figure step out of the woods and squat by the pond for a drink of water just the way I was. And we looked at each other. For a moment... for a moment I thought it was my brother Gunnar. I was sure of it. We both stood up. I even waved at him. I tell you, the hairs were standing up on my neck I was so amazed."

"But it was a Skraeling, wasn't it?"

Finn glanced toward the bluff. "Yes, I suppose it was. Let's keep moving."

"What makes ye think they're so friendly?" said Red as they began walking.

"Well, he did wave back," said Finn.

"The one ye saw might have been friendly," said Red, "but who knows about the others."

Finn shrugged. "Who knows if we'll see them again, anyway."

They climbed up through the woods and reached the top of the high bluff.

"That's it," whispered Finn. "Down there is where I saw him." He got down on his belly and Red did the same. They wriggled to the edge of the bluff and looked over. Below them lay a steep rocky slope with woods at its foot. Far beyond was the surface of the pond, placid and blue and unruffled by a breeze where it was open, a smooth frosty darkness where ice still covered it. They scanned the edge of the pond. Finn felt his breathing calm. It seemed that they were the only two living creatures as far as the eye could see.

They looked at each other, nodded, and stood up. "Well, looks like there's nae a soul there now," said Red. But as he said the words, Finn heard a twig snap behind them. He turned, his heart hammering and the hair prickling the back of his neck. Before them stood six creatures, wild-looking two-legged animals with hair festooned with feathers. They were clad in dark leather clothes and poked long spears at them. But they didn't stand for long. They rushed forward, quiet as air. Everything that happened next seemed to happen in silence to Finn. He saw the wild men lunging toward him. He took an instinctive step backward as the realization struck home that these creatures were not beasts, they were Skraelings, Skraelings even wilder than the one he'd seen the day before. He felt something pulling him backward and the wild men vanished and the sky flew into his eyes and then he felt himself turning over and the trees flew past him upside down and he hit the earth hard and rolled and tumbled. He could not breathe. Then everything was still, though his head was spinning. He lay on his stomach on a rocky slope, looking first at a rock with flecks that flashed in the sunlight and then up at the bluff against the sky. He'd been up there moments ago. He knew he had to flee. He also knew that he had to help Red. But he could not help Red if he didn't have a weapon.

The Tree

Woods. Streams. Thickets. Hills. More woods. More thickets.

The sun was lowering. A breeze had puffed up, the air was getting cold, and overhead the sky had turned white. Finn was worried. Nothing looked familiar. On the hike into the woods he had tried to mark the trail in his mind, but now every tree, every swamp that he passed looked alike.

A stand of immense pines loomed before him. Haven't I seen these before? he thought. Then he felt it: a rush of panic. His heart began racing and visions of wandering in circles endlessly and wild men with feathers in their hair swirled through his mind.

"Get a hold of yourself," he said out loud, his voice booming in the quiet and reverberating in his ears.

He thought that if he had brought Wulf, he would never have gotten lost.

Or if he had the sunstone.

If only he could get his bearings, see where he was, maybe he stood a chance of finding his way back. But where could he get such a view?

He eyed the trees. Yes, climbing a tree was his only chance. It would be like climbing the mast for a view.

He selected one with the lowest dead branches and began clawing his way upward. The going was easier than he expected as he clambered up the ladderlike limbs. Upward he went, scraping his skin against the bark and sticking to the oozing sap. He paused for a moment and looked down. The woods floor below looked miles away. He took a deep breath and looked upward. The sky seemed closer, but he could not yet see to either side of him because of the thick needles of the other pines.

Then he heard it: a voice. It was one word, a word that he did not understand, but there was no mistake. Someone had spoken.

He held still in his perch aloft. He tried to quiet his breathing and the juddering of his heart. He peered down through the pine boughs. He heard another voice, and another voice answer the first.

Then he saw them.

Below, passing the tree in which he clung, was a band of Skraelings. Then he caught a flash of brilliant red hair.

It was Red!

They passed by like shadows. He never heard a footstep.

He held his breath for as long as he could. Then he forced himself to wait longer to give them extra time to move away, and only then did he scramble to the crown of the tree. It swayed under his weight, and he knew it would not hold long. The breeze was stronger up here. The air was colder still. A change was coming.

But he held on long enough to see the glimmer of the sea in the distance, the long curve of the cove, and the swerve of the peninsula that separated the cove from the waters to the west that they had yet to explore. There, the sun was setting, looking like a dull bronze ball sinking into the gray water.

He shimmied down the great pine as fast as he dared, scraping and gouging his hands and face as he did.

Soon his feet hit the welcome firmness of the pine needles on the forest floor, and he was off, sprinting in the direction he had marked in his mind.

cracking

"We cannot leave until daybreak," said Leif. "To set out into the woods to rescue Red tonight would risk too many men's lives. Besides, Red will figure out a way to escape if anyone can. Or at least keep himself out of harm's way till we find him tomorrow."

"If we find him at all," grumbled Kormak.

Finn was exhausted. He lay on his sleeping bench almost too tired to move.

He caught Leif's eye for a moment. Leif fixed him with a cold look and raised an eyebrow. Finn could not hold his gaze and looked away. If they hadn't sneaked off on such a foolhardy escapade, Red would be standing with them now.

"You've been a fool, Skald," said Leif. "You disappoint me." There was darkness in his voice. Finn forced himself to meet his gaze.

"We need you to take us to where you last saw Red,"

said Leif. "But after tomorrow, I'm confining you to the house." Leif shook his head, then turned away.

One thought tortured Finn and would not let him slip into sleep: He was the one who was responsible for Red. He had left Red to the Skraelings. It was his fault. How could he leave him alone out there for the rest of the night?

Reckless Skald indeed. The name made him feel like a fool, just as Leif had said.

Now he had lost two things precious to him: First it was the sunstone, the last object he possessed that had been touched by his father. And now Red. Where would he ever find someone like Red? Guilt flooded him when he thought back on their walk to the bluff: He felt he'd been unfair to compare Red unfavorably to Bo.

The night crept onward, and still Finn could not fall asleep. The men moved to their sleeping benches and the firelight flickered lower on the log walls. Soon the sound of snoring mingled with the crackling of the dying fire.

Over and over Finn thought about what had happened that afternoon.

He saw the Skraelings approaching, he felt himself somersault off the bluff, he heard the voices in the woods beneath his tree, he felt his heart drumming in his chest. And over and over he wondered why he had not done something to save Red.

Red had saved his life on the voyage from Greenland. Finn owed him. But he had let him down.

Finn knew why.

He turned his face away from the firelight to stare at the dark log wall. He knew why no plan of attack had sprung to mind.

He had been running for his life. He had been scared, more scared than he'd ever been. He had been so scared he could not think.

Now he was lying in a warm bed while Red was a captive somewhere out in the wilderness. His heart beat a hard cadence as he squeezed his eyes shut as much to keep away tears as to try to force himself to sleep.

Daybreak found him at the bottom of an inky well of sleep, a well so deep it took a solid shove from Leif to rouse him. He pulled on his warm tunic and grabbed a piece of dried salmon. Except for three sentries and Kormak, who would stay behind, the men had already gathered outside in the dove-gray light. They were armed with swords and broadaxes and spears.

"Lead the way," said Leif softly, just as a snowflake swooped by like a frozen moth. It was followed by another, and another after that. Finn saw Leif and Sven glance at each other. He knew what that meant: If it snowed hard, they would not be able to track the Skraelings.

They moved fast, but the snow moved faster. Fine

flakes began to whisper down with a dense, rhythmic intensity, filling the woods with inch after inch of powder.

The men did not speak, so the only sounds were the occasional crack of a branch, the creak of their leather shoes against the snow, and the hush of the falling snowflakes.

By the time they'd reached the bluff at mid-morning, the snow fell so hard the pond below lay gray and indistinct. The frozen section was covered in white.

"This is where they were," whispered Finn. "They came up right behind us. We never knew they were there."

They stood for a long moment. Leif surveyed the pond, then turned to consider the woods.

"Take us to the pine where you last saw Red."

Finn headed off in the direction he thought was correct, but they had walked a long way before he realized that the terrain was different from what it had been the day before. He stopped to try to get his bearings.

"Um, that way," he said, pointing toward a thick stand of spruce.

He felt Leif's hand on his shoulder.

"Finn," he said. "It's no use. We can't find our own way in this snow. What makes you think we'll find Red and the Skraelings?"

Finn looked up at Leif. Snow had frosted his beard.

"But we must find him," he said, his voice cracking.

"Yes, we must, Finn," he said. "But not now. We'll have to wait till the snow stops falling. Then we can head out to try to intersect their path. But right now it'll be everything we can do just to find our way back."

Finn looked upward to see the rapid descent of countless flakes. Snow wet his nose and caught in his eyelashes and batted at his cheeks.

Leif took his hand off Finn's shoulder and strode away into the woods. The men slowly followed. Finn wanted to call out to Red, to hear his voice echo through the voiceless woods, and to hear Red's voice echo in return.

But instead he wiped the snow from his face and turned to follow.

deep into the woods

The snow did not stop falling for two days. When a pale blue sky finally showed above the crumbling snow clouds, a small band of Vikings went after Red. Leif made Finn stay behind to cut firewood and tend to the animals.

At dusk on the second day the men returned. The sentry called out and everyone ran outside to greet them. One by one they emerged from the woods, each of them looking weary and tense. Then Leif and another Viking pushed their way into the clearing—Sven supported between them, his arms slung over their shoulders. His broad face was white as the snow. His right leg was wrapped with a bloodstained rag.

Other Vikings helped Sven inside and lay him before the fire. A cup of hot broth was thrust into his hands.

"That wound must be cleaned out and dressed," said Leif. "Get me hot water and bandages."

He kneeled in front of Sven and dipped a rag into a bowl of hot water. He took the cup of broth out of his hands and then daubed at the wound. Sven flinched and gasped.

"You've lost a lot of blood, Sven," he said. "And it's still bleeding."

"I'll...be...all...right," said Sven in a thin, gravelly voice. He grimaced. He turned his gaze to Finn as Finn and Wulf stood beside him. His eyes were glassy.

"What happened?" said Finn, resting his hand on Wulf's back as Wulf nuzzled Sven.

"We were far into land we'd not yet explored," said Leif, "off beyond the far hills. We made camp. We'd seen no sign of Skraelings. Dawn was clear, and with it came the Skraelings, rushing in on us like the wind. They paid for their boldness. We killed three of them. But a Skraeling caught Sven in the leg with a hatchet."

Finn looked at Sven. Now his eyes were half-closed. A cold realization hit him: Sven was sinking fast.

"Was...was there any sign of Red?"

Leif looked into the fire and shook his head.

"Not that we could see," he said. He looked at Finn. "No, there was no sign of him. And now it's too risky to keep searching for him." He looked at Sven and then stared at the fire.

Sven let out a low groan.

"Let him rest now," said Leif. The men drifted away. Finn went to his sleeping bench and watched Leif and

Sven. The firelight dancing and throwing shadows on the walls was all that moved.

Finn watched until Leif's head drooped and nodded. Yes, he would keep watching. Sven would rest, perhaps rest until he passed into the next world. His face had turned gray, lit pale pink on his cheeks by the firelight. Leif was exhausted, that Finn knew. But Finn would keep watching. He would keep watching until he knew Leif was deep in sleep. He knew what he had to do.

Finn and Wulf churned through the snow till the dark shape of the house dropped away behind them. Yes, he was going to find Red. He couldn't bear the thought that Red might be suffering like Sven. True, Red might already be dead or carried off to some distant territory beyond Finn's reach. Just as he had been carried off by Vikings from his home island, now he'd been carried off from his adopted family by the Skraelings. But Finn knew he had to try again to find him.

They came to a clearing. Before them stood a small herd of deer. The deer bolted. Wulf raced off after them, disappearing into a thick stand of pine on the other side of the clearing. The pine branches nodded and finally fell still. Finn called and called, but Wulf would not come back.

He followed the tracks into the woods. Deeper and deeper into the woods he went. The snow was fluffy and easy enough to walk through, but Finn grew more and more tense the farther he got from the houses.

The world grew still. Finn kept calling out as he trotted in Wulf's tracks, even though he didn't want to let anything—or anyone—know he was there.

An orange half moon pushed its way above the spiked top of the pines. Soon it rose high enough to light Finn's way. He could see his breath rising like smoke in the moonlight. He looked at the moon. It was the one with the tilted face of a sad boy, or a seal pup peering out of the water. How many different faces the moon had! It was if it changed masks as it waxed and waned.

Owls began to *hoo-hoo, hoo-hoo-hoo* to each other. Finn knew that wolves lived in the woods, but he was not going to leave Wulf alone—even if the pup had run away. He knew that Red was out there somewhere and he was going to find him. He was not about to lose Wulf, too.

Finn climbed a low hill. "Wulf!" he called. "Wulf, come back here now!" The moonlight made the snow cover twinkle with tiny pink, blue, and silver gems. At the top of the hill the trees thinned out. Below stretched the same pond he had seen with Red the day the Skraelings attacked them. Now ice covered its entire surface.

What Finn spotted out at the edge of the ice made him drop to the snow and scramble on all fours to a bush for cover.

CHAPTER 19

a small campfire

Skraelings, thought Finn. Fear cut through him. Among a stand of pine and birch at the edge of the pond, he could see a small campfire burning, a flicker of gold and orange flame in the gloom. It must be Skraelings, he thought. He knew he should turn and run as fast as he could back to safety. He knew he should forget about Wulf—the pup was old enough to fend for himself—but he could not bear the thought of leaving his dog alone in the woods.

Maybe, just maybe, Red was with the Skraelings.

Still, he didn't want to be caught by the Skraelings. What would they do to him if they caught him? He shivered. He thought of the salmon the men had filleted and dried on racks. Would the Skraelings do that to him? Had they already skinned Red?

But why had the first Skraeling he'd seen appear to be friendly?

The image of Sven, his face as white as birch bark,

appeared before him. His eyes were closed and there was frost on his beard. It took Finn's breath away.

He must have died, he thought. He will not see Greenland's shores again.

He had no more time to dwell on Sven's fate. From out of the woods beside the pond Wulf burst onto the ice. He ran on a line toward the fire. Finn stared in horror. What could he do? Should he jump up and run after him? Why wouldn't Wulf listen before? Why was he running away now?

He was thinking that he'd failed as a dog trainer when he heard something rustle behind him and he began to stand up and turn around.

A figure separated itself from the dark form of a pine and hurtled toward him.

It's happening again, he thought. They've tricked me again.

He didn't have time to open his mouth or raise his hands in defense before the figure lunged at him and hit him square in the stomach. He fell backward, breathless, and landed in the snow. He kicked and swung his fists, catching his assailant on one ear. But the man seemed oblivious to pain and gripped Finn by the throat.

"Easy, there," said the man. But Finn, crazy with fright, kept struggling. He swung and hit the man's ear again. "Hey, stop that," said the man again. "Who are you? You're no Skraeling."

It took a moment for Finn to realize that he was hearing his own language. And it was a voice that he knew as well as his own.

He looked up at the figure looming over him. The moonlight glinted off an object dangling from his neck.

It was a carved ivory chess piece, a warrior.

"Gunnar?" panted Finn. "Is that you, Gunnar?"

The man eased his grip from Finn's neck. He said nothing for a moment.

Then he stood up, gripped Finn by his shoulders, plucked him off the ground, and stood him up before him.

Before he could say anything, someone else rushed up from behind Finn.

"What in the name of thunder do we have here?" Finn heard a gravelly voice bellow. It was a voice that could only belong to one person in all the world.

Olaf Farseeker, his father.

Reunion

The moon hung bright and the night held its breath. All was stillness and dark tree shapes, lanes of moonlight and pulsing starlight.

But the three Vikings clung to each other in the moon glow, smoke from their breath drifting upward. They were clapping each other on the back, laughing, and firing questions at each other.

"How did you get here?" Olaf said. "By thunder, we could have killed you, boy! Sneaking up on us like that!"

"I sailed with Leif the Lucky," said Finn, floating with happiness. "We hit storms and fog and built houses when we landed and I saw the ribs of *Dragonwing* and..."

"And your mother approved?" growled Olaf. "Did she allow you to sail?"

"Well, Father...I..."

Olaf gripped Finn by the shoulders. He leaned down and pressed his nose into Finn's, making the cartilage crack. Finn could feel the bristles of his wiry beard tickle his face.

"You disobeyed me, then," he said, lowering his voice to a growl. Finn felt the elation drain away. He was suddenly a child again. How was it that only a few words from his father could crush him? Perhaps it was because he knew his father was right. He knew he had betrayed him—and his mother.

But then Olaf threw his arms around him. "But you're the best thing that's happened to us in a year," he said, laughing again. "You found us in the kingdom of the lost. We'll deal with you breaking your word to me later."

"It was a good thing we heard you calling for your dog," said Gunnar. "Father said, 'That's no Skraeling, that's a Viking.' I wasn't so sure myself. But the way my ear hurts now, I'm sure it was a Viking."

They laughed.

Gunnar clapped Finn hard on the back. "Let me look at you," he said, gripping him by the shoulders and holding him at arm's length. "Yes, little brother," he said, beaming, "I never thought the sight of you could bring me such joy."

"Better keep it quiet," said Olaf, looking around him. "The Skraelings are close by. We saw a band of them just off to the north. They're moving back down this way from the northern coast. Let's break camp and go hoist a horn with Leif. Didn't I tell you I thought some of our own people would have come here by now, Gunnar?"

Olaf laughed again and draped his arm over Finn's shoulders as they started down the hill to the pond.

"This'll go down as one of the best days in history," he said. "Do you how long we've been living out in these woods? Hoping we were going in one direction when the Skraelings were going in the other? Since we made our unfortunate landing on this coast last summer, first we headed north, a two-week walk, to the rocky shores where we wintered. We wanted to escape the Skraelings we'd fought down here. But at least the game was plentiful near our camp. We've only just arrived back in this land to winter here, where the snow might not be as deep. The Skraelings move from place to place and we decided to risk coming back here in the hope that they had left for other regions. Let me tell you, it gets tiresome, dodging Skraelings and wondering if you'll ever get home."

"I saw *Dragonwing*," said Finn. "I thought I might never see you ..."

"We ran aground in the dirtiest blow you've ever seen," said Olaf, his voice quieter now. "Ran aground and lost ... many ..." He cleared his throat. "We lost many men." He looked at Finn.

"Einar was taken by the sea," he said, now almost whispering to himself. "*Dragonwing* was lost. We ran aground in a storm. Half the crew drowned. And Einar ..."

His voice caught. He blinked and looked at Finn. "Einar was lost to the waves."

Finn felt a kind of dizziness come over him. At the same time, something was happening inside his chest. A feeling like moths fluttering overswept him. It was the same feeling he had when he saw Sven brought back from the dark woods.

"And the Skraelings killed everyone else, brave lads that they were," said Olaf. "You knew them all, Finn. Six of them, killed in battle, fighting with heart and fire. We thought we could defeat these Skraelings, but I'll tell you, they're tough. They know the land, and they fight like devils. The ones who fight, that is. There were others later on who helped us, Gunnar and me, gave us food in exchange for some of the small pieces of amber we had with us."

They approached the campfire in silence. Finn did not know what to say. The feeling of fluttering gave way to a heaviness in his arms and legs and chest, and a burning feeling in his eyes and heart. Einar, his brother who was so much like his father, was gone. The men he'd known since he was a boy, gone.

Wulf came bounding over the ice to greet them.

"So, this must be your pup, eh, Finn?" said Olaf, gripping his young son's shoulder ever tighter.

journey by moonlight

They doused the campfire, rolled up the tent, and headed into the woods.

"Lead on," said Olaf to Finn. "You know the way." He clapped Finn on the back. Finn grinned and began retracing his moonlit footprints. But then he thought of Red.

"Before we head back," he said, "I must tell you about Red." He told his father and brother the story of Red's capture, the first search, and the second search that brought about Sven's wound.

"And you, you decided to seek him yourself?" said Olaf with disbelief in his voice.

"Yes, Father. Leif was too exhausted to go again. I knew I had to go. I was afraid that we might never find him."

Olaf considered his son for a moment. "This is what we'll do," he said. "You take us back to Leif's camp so we can get some food and get warm. Then we'll rally old Leif and search for your redheaded friend."

Finn beamed. "Thank you, Father."

The rhythm of their pace kept the fatigue from their legs. The walk began to make Finn feel as though he were flying just above ground level. The sky seemed immovable above him. He felt suspended between earth and sky. Now and then he turned to see the moonlit figures of Gunnar and Olaf following. Wulf stayed at his heels.

A grayish light the color of a dove's wing began to grow in the east as the moon coasted toward the horizon.

Soon Finn began smelling a new smell, a smell different from the pine pitch and fragrance of the fir needles that had filled his nostrils on their walk through the forest. This was the scent of the sea.

Now they were almost there.

Just over the next hill, then down the beach—it wasn't much farther. He began walking faster. How wonderful it would be to arrive with his father and brother in tow! Alas, his brother Einar was lost, along with the rest of the crew. Red was still off in the wilderness. But Finn, at last, had found his father and Gunnar.

The scent of wood smoke came to him on the cold air.

"I smell a Viking cooking breakfast," whispered Olaf. "And by thunder I'm ready to eat."

Wintry lavender light had begun to seep into the sky when Finn, Gunnar, and Olaf—with Wulf now trotting in the lead—walked into the settlement. One of the Vikings stepped out from behind a tree, sword drawn. "Halt! Who goes there?" he roared.

"It is Finn, and Father and Gunnar! I've found the Farseekers!" shouted Finn.

In a moment the doorways of the houses spilled out Viking after Viking.

Fur hat askew, Leif surged out, pulling a deerskin robe around him.

"What's this I hear? Finn has returned?"

"With Olaf Farseeker!" cried a Viking.

Leif strode over and embraced Olaf.

"Truth be told, Olaf," he said, "I'd about given you up for dead." He lay his hand on Finn's shoulder.

"We'd about given ourselves up for dead," laughed Olaf.

Kormak sauntered out. "Well, so I lose my bet," he said to Finn. "The Skraelings didn't eat you after all. But they did get Sven and Red."

Olaf shot him a look. "I remember you, Kormak. Leif, why is he sailing with you? I've always heard that his ravens couldn't find a roost if they were sitting on it."

"Alas, worthy ravenkeepers are as rare as ever," said Leif. "For all he's done for us, he might as well have stayed home. It was your son and his sunstone that helped us find the way."

Finn glanced at Kormak. Kormak glanced at him, and

in his dark look Finn read the truth. Kormak looked away and muttered, "I should have stayed home." He turned and went back inside.

Finn said, "Leif, tell me. How is Sven?"

Leif turned to him. "Finn," he said in a softer voice. "Sven died just before dawn. He is no longer suffering. We have lost a brave and faithful Viking. We will bury him today."

Leif turned to Olaf and Gunnar. "We have lost my mate Sven and also our ship's boy, a young Scot named Red. But I will tell you all in due time. My friends, let's get you into the warmth and get something inside you to cheer your spirits. You must rest and tell us of your adventures."

olaf's story

Olaf, Gunnar, Leif, and Finn ate in silence as the crewmen served them plate after plate of venison and partridge. Once Olaf had eaten his fill, he said, "No sight more wonderful have I seen than the face of Finn in the moonlight." He glanced at Finn. Finn felt heat rush to his cheeks. A thought also rushed through his mind: What would it be like now that his father had returned? I was on my own, he thought, and now, in my father's eyes, I'm just a little boy again.

The smile left Olaf's face. "But many terrible things I have been forced to see before I saw my youngest son again."

He cleared his throat. The Vikings quieted down and turned to listen. The fire crackled, and sparks showered upward as a log shifted.

"We made a fair crossing," said Olaf, moving to a bench closer to the fire. He settled back against a rough-hewn post. He motioned to Finn and Gunnar to sit beside him.

"The men were in good spirits and the skies smiled on us," he said. "But then, a day beyond the land of golden sands..."

"We called it Wonderstrand," said Leif.

"And a fine name it is," said Olaf. "A day beyond Wonderstrand, the breeze backed around to the north-east. It whipped into a blow of such fury that one of my men threw himself overboard rather than face what he believed was certain drowning in *Dragonwing*.

"We lost the mast just as we were losing daylight the second day of the blow. The waves reared three times the height of the prow, cruel green waves that clawed and hammered at the ship. Heavy breakers tumbled across the deck. We might have made it if we hadn't run aground. Just to the north of here, the waters off the coast are very foul, a wilderness of sandbars and shoals. On one of these we ran hard aground, and the seas made short work of our valiant vessel.

"The worst part was that we could see the beach not far off through the spume and spray. 'Shall we swim for it?' Einar asked me. The ship was listing, the groan and crack of breaking strakes was in my ears, the waves were pounding us to shreds. 'Follow me!' I yelled. I grabbed a line and leaped into the water. The last I heard of Einar was his great roar of a laugh from somewhere behind me."

He stopped and lowered his voice. The firelight flickered in his eyes. "From then on I lost contact with everyone. The water tried to swallow me. I could not see the shore, I could not see the ship, I could not see Einar or Gunnar or anyone else. But somehow the waves did not want me—perhaps they had their fill with Einar and the others—and I swam like a drowning puppy through the waves. I found myself gasping on the beach, the waves curling around my feet. A lump of a figure washed up not far away, and I crawled over. It was Gunnar, by thunder. Six others made it to shore. But no one else survived. The sea gave no other bodies to us. I called for Einar over the crash and boom and hiss of the waves, but no one answered."

When he fell silent, the only sound in the room was the crackle of the fire.

"From there we built a shelter from the planks of the ship," he continued. "We built it deep in the forest so we would not be seen. We knew we were in trouble—no tools to build another ship, no food, no weapons but for our knives. But we managed to put together a shelter. With our knives we made spears and arrows and bows. Soon we were able to hunt and fish. But not long after came the night the Skraelings came to visit.

"They appeared without warning one evening when the sun was nearing the horizon. There was a large band of them, maybe twenty, twenty-five. They wore feathers in their long black hair and they carried bows and arrows, spears, and axes. They seemed not to be afraid of us, but moved into our camp quickly. One of them began talking loudly, angrily, as if he was demanding something, gesturing and pointing. One of our men, Thorvald, must have gotten spooked and panicked, for he drew his knife and yelled, 'Get out of our camp!'

"Never in my days have I seen anyone move so swiftly as the Skraelings. No sooner had Thorvald uttered his words than three arrows—one, two, three, one right after the other—took him in the chest and quivered there. He dropped to his knees, then fell over sideways, already dead. I pushed Gunnar behind the shelter and told him to run into the forest. By the time I turned back to help the others it was too late. One had been shot with arrows and the other was on his back, set on by two Skraelings who were finishing him with their spears. The others were knifed and lay dying of their wounds.

"No, I did not rush them. I did not throw myself to certain death at their hands. Perhaps that would have been the honorable act, but I knew no man by himself, armed only with a knife, not even a Viking, could live alone for long out there. I had to join Gunnar. I owed it to my eldest son to try to survive together."

He paused to drink deeply from a horn of beer. He

wiped his lips. "My, now that's a taste of heaven," he said. "Beer was something we could only dream of through the long days and nights, as were many of the comforts of home. We learned to sneak, to track the animals, to know where the Skraelings were, and to stay out of their way. We figured that we would be in this land a long time. If not forever."

He took another swig and wiped his mouth on his sleeve.

"Yes, our shelter protected us, but the Skraelings were too close," he said. "So we struck off far to the north and found a long rock-strewn peninsula where the game was plentiful. But the winter was harsh there, and soon even the game grew scare. We lived on dried venison and the shellfish we dug along the beaches. We decided that wintering here was worth the risk of running into the Skraelings who had attacked us.

"To this day I blame myself for the attack," he said, his voice lowering. "I should have stopped Thorvald, and maybe he and the others would be with us now. For we found some other Skraelings who were willing to trade food and furs for our amber. Maybe the first band would not have attacked if..."

When he fell silent this time, Leif said, "You must be tired, Olaf. Why not rest and tell us more later. You've done a Viking's job of telling how you found this new land, this land we call Wineland. Now I know where Finn the Reckless Skald got his gift."

Olaf grinned at Finn. "Yes, that's something I've not heard in too long a time. A poem from my young skald's heart." He turned to Leif. "My story's told, skipper, but for the part where under a moonlit sky we thought we were being tracked by a Skraeling—a Skraeling who turned out to be the Reckless Skald."

Finn had been watching his father, absorbed in his story. I will put this in a poem someday, he thought. This will be a saga that all Vikings will remember.

farewell to sven

In the crystal light of morning the men cleared the snow away from a hillside overlooking the sea and set to digging Sven's grave.

The ground had frozen only a few inches deep. By the time the sun rode above the crowns of the spruces, the men had cleared away the snow and dug a deep grave and lined it with rocks. Only the wind whispering in the spruce boughs, the gulls crying above the waves, and the murmuring waves themselves made any comment as the men brought Sven's body up from the house and laid it in the earth.

Leif kneeled beside the grave and set Sven's spear, knife, and the small harp down in the grave beside the body.

"May you travel well," said Leif, straightening up. His voice was low and gravelly. "Play your harp when you get to heaven, wherever it may be. You have been a fine and faithful friend, and we will miss you."

Leif turned and walked down the hill. The men set to shoveling the dirt and rocks over Sven. When they finished, they piled rocks on top of the grave. Then they straggled back down the hill to the house. Finn, Olaf, and Gunnar lingered.

After a silence, Olaf said, "Leif and Sven have been friends since they were boys. Sven was a true-hearted Viking, but I expect Leif will learn to get along without him."

"He doesn't have much choice," said Gunnar. "It's just as we have had to learn to get along without Einar."

Finn looked out at the blue sea sparkling in the sun. How swift the passage seemed between this life and the next, he thought, as swift as passing from the surface of the sea to the depths beneath.

"Already too many men have died on this expedition," said Olaf. "The bounty here is not worth the price. We need to go home and, if we return, bring three ships. We need many Vikings to help us face the dangers of this land."

"Father, but what about Red?"

Olaf turned to his son. "How many times have you gone to hunt for him? Sven died trying. And even though you've combed these woods, there's been no sign of him." He sighed. "Finn, I know how you feel. But the danger is too great. Leif and I talked this over. There is no way we can hunt for him. The danger is too great."

"But he saved my life. I owe him mine."

"Not," said Olaf, "if he is already dead."

Finn felt a bitterness surge into his heart. How could his father do this? He'd not been back a day and already he was telling Finn what to do. Finn knew that his father was trying to help, but the feeling remained: He resented his father horning in.

Finn blinked and looked away. His father had said the words that he would not say to himself but which haunted him. Red, he realized, had probably been killed within the first few hours of his capture. But he could not be certain.

"Let's go back," said Olaf. "We need to discuss plans with Leif."

They walked slowly down the hill. Finn stopped and looked back at the grave.

"Thank you, Sven," he said out loud. "Thank you for giving me Wulf, and thank you for helping me, and for being kind to Red."

cold heart, true heart

"This voyage has been a disaster," grumbled Kormak. He sat before the fire holding a horn of beer. "I told you stowaways were unlucky. Now Red is gone, Sven is dead, and look what happened to Olaf and his crew."

"None of this has anything to do with stowaways," said Leif. "These are the risks you face when you undertake a great voyage."

"A great voyage?" said Kormak. "You call spending the winter in a land of desolation among monsters who want to kill you a great voyage? We haven't even done what we came here to do, to trade with the Skraelings. Where are all the furs and riches? I tell you, we cannot head for home fast enough. This will be one of the great voyages, all right—the greatest disaster of a voyage in Viking history."

"We're not here to argue, Kormak," said Olaf. "We're here to drink to Sven, not to listen to you spout off because you're afraid of the Skraelings." Finn saw a flicker of fire in his father's eye.

"Olaf's right," said Leif. "Kormak, if you want to pick a fight, go pick one with a goat."

Kormak glared. "All right, I will," he said. He gulped down the rest of his beer. He stalked to the door and went outside, leaving the door open.

Leif shook his head. "Will someone close that door? We'll discuss what to do and take a vote whether to stay or sail for home before the cove freezes us in. But before that, we must remember our friend."

He stood up and hoisted his horn toward the ceiling. Everyone stood and did the same.

"To Sven, then," he said. "To a great and good-hearted Viking. *Sea Sword* will be empty without you."

The men—Finn included—drank deeply from their horns.

Everyone sat back down. Wulf wandered over to Finn and whimpered. Finn began scratching him behind the ears. He thought how everything had changed. When he'd arrived, the new land was full of the promise of discovery and excitement. Now it had become a different land, one of sadness, fear, and death.

How could he leave his friend in such a place? Red must still be alive—he could not bring himself to utter the other possibility to himself. But if they left Wineland now, there'd be no hope for Red.

The mystery of Red, he thought. This is something else I'll need to put into a poem.

And the moment he thought about using Red's fate as something to be used in a poem, he did not like himself. There was something coldhearted about it. There was something mean-spirited and aloof, as if he were a vulture, floating above everything, watching, waiting.

But whether he liked himself for it or not, he knew it was true: The life he saw around him, good or bad, was the subject of his poems. This was his true heart.

Wulf whimpered again.

"What is it, boy?" said Finn. "What's bothering you? What do you want?"

Then he smiled.

"Ah, I know what it is."

Finn cupped his hand and poured some beer into it. He let Wulf lap it up. Wulf looked up at him in gratitude. He licked his hand dry.

"Want some more?" said Finn, and Wulf wagged his tail.

It was then that the door flew open, and Kormak pounded inside, panting.

"What is it, man?" said Leif.

Gasping, Kormak cried, "Skraelings! Skraelings are everywhere!"

encounter in the snow

"Stay here!" shouted Olaf to Finn. "If there's to be bloodshed, I want you somewhere safe."

"But Father..." said Finn as he moved to the doorway.

His father shot him a look that silenced him.

"Can you heed my words for once?" he hissed. "Stay put as I ask."

Finn felt the sting of resentment again as he stepped aside to let the Vikings with their spears and swords and axes plunge outside. His father and Gunnar followed, and Finn stood at the doorway, peering out.

Already there was a band of Skraelings gathered before the clearing, and others were stepping out of the woods to join them. Their black hair was festooned with feathers. They wore necklaces of bear claws and bear teeth. They carried spears and bows and arrows. Their faces were painted with red stripes. They did not smile.

"I cannot tell if these are the same Skraelings who attacked us before," whispered Olaf to Leif. "But we'd better be ready. They might not have murdered our crew, but they look like they're ready for a fight."

The Vikings formed a line, their weapons at the ready. No one said a word. Footsteps creaked on the snow. A breeze hustled through the pines.

"We're outnumbered. I don't want any trouble," said Leif to Olaf. "Let's see if we can barter with them."

Olaf scowled. "They'd sooner kill us than trade with us, that I can tell you."

"We must try," said Leif as he stepped forward.

"We come from across the sea," he said, gesturing toward the ship in the cove. "We come to trade with you. Though you have done our people harm, we will trade with you. We will not take revenge for your deeds."

One of the Skraelings stepped forward and said something in his own language.

Gunnar turned to Leif. "Look at the sleds. They brought furs to trade. But even if these are not the people who killed our men, I'd sooner trade sword blows with them than furs."

"Gunnar, look around you," said Leif. "How many of them do you count? And how many of us? We have no choice."

Leif told the men to bring out the trading goods.

"Things aren't looking too promising," he said. "I didn't come here to be massacred."

Finn, watching from the doorway, felt his heart hammering in his chest. Would there be a fight?

He surveyed the band of Skraelings. There . . . yes, standing to the side was the young Skraeling he had seen at the pond. He now wore feathers in his hair, but there was no mistaking him—he looked like Gunnar's twin brother.

The Vikings brought out a small chest. Leif kneeled down and opened the lid. Inside were gleaming bracelets and necklaces made of silver and amber. One of the Skraelings pushed the bale of furs over to the Vikings, and then the Skraelings took turns taking a treasure from the chest.

When they were finished, Leif closed the lid. He pointed at the bale of furs, then pointed at the chest. Then he held up two fingers.

"Another bale of fur and you can have another turn at the chest," he said.

A Viking came from the shed with a bucket of fresh milk and a dipper. A few Skraelings sipped it, then chattered to each other. Out from the woods a Skraeling brought another bale of furs, and the Skraelings lined up for the milk.

"Don't let your guard down," said Leif. He ran his

fingers through the dense fur of one of the pelts. "Give them more milk, and then let's get these furs inside. I don't like being outnumbered."

a man's job

When the Skraelings had drunk the last of the milk, they gathered their silver and amber jewelry and slipped back into the woods. The Vikings watched them go. Finn knew the Skraeling he'd recognized had not seen him waiting in the house, and he wanted to call out to him. But all the Skraelings had disappeared into the woods.

Olaf said, "Next time, they might just decide to take everything and give us nothing but trouble in return."

They turned to go into the house, but before a single Viking could step across the threshold, they heard the cow mooing from the shed. She was mooing hard and fast and loud. Then the goats began bleating. The ravens joined in with angry croaking.

"Something's wrong," said Olaf. He sprinted toward the shed. Finn watched him go. For a moment, he stood still, but then it was as if an invisible force drew him across the threshold onto the snow.

Finn followed Olaf, and when he came around the side of the pen, he saw five Skraelings. One of them was tugging on a rope tied around the cow's neck. One opened the pen and shooed the goats out. The ravens were on their perch, flapping and croaking.

"What do you think you're doing?" cried Olaf, reaching for his sword. One of the Skraelings drew an arrow from his quiver, set it in his bow, and drew back the bowstring. He let the arrow fly. The arrow flicked through the air and buried itself in Olaf's shoulder. He dropped his sword and fell to his knees, the arrow lodged deep in his flesh.

The Skraelings pulled the cow out of the shed and began running into the woods, pulling the cow after them. The ravens flapped off into the woods. The goats had already disappeared.

Finn's mind went blank. At first he felt weightless. He couldn't move. But then he saw himself running to Olaf's side. He saw Olaf's sword. He saw himself picking it up and gripping it with two hands. He saw himself rushing at the Skraelings. He was screaming a scream like a flight of a thousand eagles. He raised the sword and saw Wulf flash in front of him to leap at one of the Skraelings. He saw the Skraelings moving toward the woods—except for the one whose arrow was lodged in his father's shoulder. He was running back toward Olaf.

Then, beside him, he saw Kormak running. Kormak was yelling, "You stole my ravens! Come back with them!" He dodged right past the Skraeling.

Finn ran toward the Skraeling. The Skraeling was nearing Olaf. Olaf lay on the snow gripping the arrow in his shoulder. But Finn didn't swing his sword. He lunged at the Skraeling's legs and tackled him, flipping him end over end. The Skraeling flopped onto the snow. He spun around with a look of hatred and horror in his eyes. He drew his knife. The blade flashed upward.

As if in a dream, Finn saw over the Skraeling's shoulder a little bird hop onto a pine bough, tilt its black cap at him, and whir away, causing snow to sift down.

But the blade never came down. Finn heard someone yell—a Skraeling. The knife remained frozen to the sky as he looked around. There, by the woods, stood the Skraeling who looked like Gunnar. The Skraeling yelled some more words that Finn did not understand, but whatever they were, they made the Skraeling with the knife stand up, thrust the knife into its sheath, and turn and run away.

Finn looked around to see Leif kneeling by Olaf. When he turned back to look for the Skraeling, there was nothing but woods.

Leif put his hands underneath Olaf's back and helped him sit up. Olaf was clutching his shoulder. The arrow jutted out of it and rose and fell as he breathed. The shoulder of his tunic was bright and wet with blood.

Finn found himself leaning over his father, resting his hand on his broad back.

"The gods have finally granted us some small favor," said Olaf, his voice quavery and hoarse. His face was turning pale. "You, Finn. You did well. Very well indeed." He stopped to catch his breath. "That was a man's job you did back there. You stopped the Skraeling." He grimaced and whispered, "You saved my life." Then he managed a chuckle. "Even though you disobeyed me again. Your mother," he said, coughing, "your mother named you well."

Wulf trotted over and licked Olaf on the cheek.

Now everyone had gathered. There were shouts from the Vikings, calls for revenge, but Leif raised his hand for silence.

"We are not going to rush into the woods like fools again," he said. "Already Olaf has lost too many men, and now we too have suffered losses. We'll stand our ground, yes, but I'll not risk another life to seek revenge. I will go after Kormak. Get Olaf back to the house. The time has come, it's clear to me, to leave this land until we can return in greater numbers."

Leif, Gunnar, and Finn helped Olaf to his feet. Finn took his father's arm and draped it over his shoulder. Olaf gave him a weak smile. As they trudged toward the house, Finn glanced once more toward the woods.

He thought of the Skraeling—and he thought of Red. The two people who had helped him had vanished almost as quickly as they had appeared in his life.

Leif's decision

Inside the house, Gunnar and Finn worked to remove the arrow from Olaf's shoulder. They had to force it all the way through the other side so they could break off the arrowhead, then extract the shaft. To help fight the pain, Olaf bit into a corner of Leif's deerskin robe while he underwent the operation. He never uttered even a moan during the whole ordeal, though he did leave deep teeth marks in the thick leather.

Leif returned not long after Finn and Gunnar had finished dressing and wrapping Olaf's wound. Leif stepped before the fire and shook his head.

"I have brought back Kormak," he said. "But the Skraelings have taken his life. He had his throat cut, so they must have ambushed him. He was a fool. A fool to rush into the woods, and he has paid the price. But now Sven will have a Viking to keep him company, like him or not."

He paused and pulled something out from his tunic.

"Finn, I found this on Kormak." He tossed a pouch to Finn. Finn caught it, opened it, and shook out the sunstone into his palm. The sunstone dropped into his palm.

"How did Kormak come to have it?" Leif asked.

Finn looked at the sunstone and then at Leif. He wanted to blurt, "Ah-ha! I knew it all along!" But he said nothing.

"I was going to tell you that it was missing," said Finn. "But I was afraid to make trouble."

Leif nodded. "I see," he said.

Leif turned to Olaf. "And you? How is the wound?"

"It will heal," he said. "I had it cared for well."

Leif sat down before the fire and sighed.

"No, I do not like to lose men, even if it was Kormak." He drew his fur hat from his head and held it in his hands.

"To wait for the season of voyages is too risky," he said. "I venture that we cannot afford to wait for the sun to ride high in the sky again. The Skraelings have taken our cow and goats. The ravens have returned to the wild. The Skraelings will be back, and we are outnumbered. When we return to Greenland, we will rally more ships, and we'll voyage once again to this rich land next season. But for now, I will not risk more lives. We will sail as soon as *Sea Sword* can be made ready."

Finn turned to look at his father. The light from the

flames flickered over his reddish beard and danced in his eyes, but he seemed to be thinking of other times, other things. Finn wondered how painful his wound must be.

The sentries posted outside that night saw or heard no sign of the Skraelings. In the morning, the Vikings buried Kormak not far from Sven, but far enough, Leif said, so they wouldn't bother each other. Then Leif led a party down to the beach and the ship and set the men to work. The men had hauled the ship far enough out of the water so they could work on the hull. They recaulked seams and resealed the strakes with pine pitch.

"Now I know why we're lucky the cove did not freeze," said Leif, inspecting the work on the ship with Olaf and Finn. "We're ready to sail." He turned to look back at the houses. "Now we must make ready for our voyage. Have the men gather game and water and pack the supplies from the houses. We'll stow as much lumber as possible. We must make haste before our Skraeling friends decide they'd rather keep us here forever."

RIDERS ON THE SEA

The sky hung low and gray. Snow would soon be falling. A steady breeze shivered over the wolf-gray water. Everyone was aboard: the crew, Olaf, Finn, Gunnar, and Wulf. Leif stood at the tiller.

"Man the oars, Vikings," he called. "It's time to shove off."

The first stroke sent *Sea Sword* surging forward into the water. The only sounds aboard the ship were the lap of water against the hull and the creak and grind and splash of the oars.

Finn felt Olaf lay a hand on his shoulder.

"We leave much behind on these shores," said his father. "But we shall return, perhaps, should the winds favor us, and make this land a Viking land."

Finn looked at the low wooded hills and the long sandy beach receding. Wineland had been an adventure, but not the adventure he had imagined.

Maybe that was what becoming a man meant, he

thought. Maybe adventures weren't anything that you could really imagine.

He peered into the stands of spruce and fir above the beach. Where was Red? Was he alive? Had he escaped, and skulked through the woods as Olaf and Gunnar had for so many months to elude the Skraelings?

One thought brought a moment's hope to him: Perhaps Red would take to Skraeling ways as he had to Viking ways. Perhaps he would festoon his hair with feathers and learn to sneak in the night like the wind itself.

And where was the Skraeling, his Skraeling brother?

But the hope thinned as *Sea Sword* left the sheltered waters of the cove. The men shipped their oars and hoisted the sail. Finn looked at the distant shore. He swallowed hard. He longed to see Red come running out of the woods and wave at them to come back for him. He watched as the ship rose on a swell. What could that be? For a moment he imagined he saw something emerge from the woods along the shoreline. He stared hard. The ship rose, then settled into the trough of the wave. No, there was nothing but woods. He blinked and looked at the empty shore. What had once been a land of promise had now become a dark realm of doom and mystery.

His father had been standing behind him in silence, but now he spoke.

"We've both left a lot behind in Wineland," he said.

"Thanks to you I did not leave my life behind." He smiled and then grimaced.

"How is your shoulder, Father?"

"Sore. But it will heal."

"That's good."

As they spoke, their breath puffed out from their mouths to be tugged and shredded by the breeze. They watched the land gradually recede.

"You've grown tall and sturdy since I last saw you, Finn. Do you know what was one of the things that kept me going while your brother and I were living out in the woods, trying to keep away from the Skraelings?"

"What, Father?"

"The thought of you and your mother safe and warm inside our home on the hillside."

They gazed at the diminishing shoreline in silence.

Then his father chuckled. "Probably at the same time I was thinking about that, you were somewhere on the ocean, heading toward us. There's no doubt about it, Finn. You're no longer the boy I left behind. You've proved yourself, and because of that I know I can depend on you all the more. And depend on you, Finn, to keep your impulses in check."

Finn had been waiting for this moment—the moment when his father would rebuke him. He held his breath.

"Your impulses, Finn, are what drove you to do a

great deed—and a selfish one," he said, his voice dropping to a low rasp. "You left your mother to fend for herself. This you cannot deny. You must always live with this knowledge, bitter as it is. Woe to you should anything have happened to her in your absence. Woe to you if she cannot find it in her heart to forgive you."

Finn let a thin stream of breath escape. His father was right. He felt the fire in his cheeks and the pain in his stomach. Yes, he had abandoned his mother, and for this he ached. Somehow he must find a way to earn his mother's forgiveness. But if he hadn't sailed with Leif, his father and brother would still be on the shore that was diminishing behind them.

His father looked at him and chuckled. "But a man must live with his mistakes as well as his triumphs. This I know myself."

His father fell silent, and looked out at the thin shoreline.

"Back there," he said, "you proved yourself to be a Viking. And for that, you've become a man in my eyes. I'll depend on you all the more, just as I have learned to rely on Gunnar. You'll be my mates now that Einar is with us no more."

Finn looked at the ridged gray water. This was a new way to be treated, especially by his father, and it meant that he had to act in a new way, too.

"Thank you, Father," he said, his voice coming out in a weak croak. He cleared his throat and turned to meet Olaf's gaze. "I'll do my best for you."

One night, Finn was standing watch with Olaf. The sky was powdered with stars and a full moon coasted high in the sky. Shreds of luminous clouds like winged spirits slipped past the moon on the back of the breeze. *Sea Sword* swam smooth and true over the hills of the sea, and the dark water glittered in the moonlight.

"It is a night such as this," said Olaf, gazing up at the sail as he held the tiller, "that can make a voyage seem worth it. All the danger, all the excitement..." he glanced at Finn, "...and all the heartbreak. But on a fair night such as this, you look up at the stars and you know a simple truth: It's good to be alive. It's good to be at sea. It's not the furs, the hunts, the new land. It's a peaceful night with your head in the stars."

Finn scratched Wulf behind the ear and searched the sky. Starlight shimmered on the backs of the waves.

"Now tell me, Reckless Skald," said Olaf. "I imagine that you have given thought to a poem in celebration of great deeds, Leif's grand voyage of exploration, how you rescued us, the skirmishes with the Skraelings. When you return to Greenland, you will be a hero, Finn the Reckless Skald, as your mother named you, who voyaged with Leif the Lucky, who sailed with the riders on the sea to a distant land. But let me remind you of something. You must always remember a simple night of shining stars if you are to be a true singer of the sea, and not just a blower of wind."

Finn nodded. "Father, sometimes it seems I think more about the small moments than the great deeds." Then his face darkened. "And now I think of my mother alone back in Greenland, wondering every minute of the day about what happened to her husband and her sons. And I think of my brother lost to the waves, and Sven and Kormak." He paused. "And my friend Red."

Olaf considered him for a moment. Then he said in a soft tone, "And so have you composed this great poem telling of our daring voyage, or have you only been singing songs to your dog?"

Finn could see Olaf flash a smile.

"Would you like to hear it?" said Finn.

"If you would do me the honor."

Finn looked up at the stars. "It is you, Father," he said, "who do me the honor of listening."

In the season of voyages
The slender steed of the sea
Sea Sword set sail
Bristling with brave brothers.
Leif the Lucky lent the lads

His hardy heart
And steered them safe
Through fearsome fogs
And seething storms
To a lonesome land,
A hunter's heaven
Where wild Skraelings steal.
We hewed our houses there
And found the Farseekers
Olaf and faithful Gunnar
Living in the land of the lost;
Skraelings spirited away our red-maned friend
And slaughtered Sven the good-hearted;
We skirmished with the Skraelings
And forced them to flee,
Though Olaf came close to being killed
And Kormak, crazed with anger,
Died, skewered by a Skraeling knife.
Many were the mighty deeds
And many the mysteries,
Like how the Skraeling saved the skald
But none so bold
As *Sea Sword*'s sure sailing
Through berg and breaker
To bring us back
To hearth and home again.

The waves washing, the ship pushing through the water, and the creak of the lines were the only sounds.

Then Olaf said in a low tone, "I see now that I have lost my little boy." He paused and looked up at the stars. "But I have gained a friend."

Then they both looked into the sky to see a shooting star streak a glowing trace above them as if to mark their course.

At night, after he finished his watch, Finn would go into the shelter and get some food and drink. Then he would call Wulf and curl up on the deck under his deerskin blanket. The stars would arc with the movement of the ship, disappearing behind the black rectangle of the sail, then reappearing as the ship topped a wave. His breath would billow upward until it was snatched away by the breeze. He would lean his head against the gently moving planks and listen to the music of the water as it rippled and surged and bubbled along the hull. He would think of keeping watch at night with Red, and the Skraeling by the pond, and his mother back home, and the skates his grandfather had given him, and the initials carved in the stem of *Dragonwing,* and all sorts of phantom thoughts like a procession of dreams.

One night he fell asleep listening to the gurgle and hum of the water. In his dream, he could see through the hull, as if it were made of clear ice, and through the ice he saw someone swimming to catch up with the ship. At first he thought it was a dolphin, but then he saw that it was Red, grinning and waving, swimming just as fast as the ship with no apparent effort. He called his name to get him to stop and talk, but Red only grinned and waved and swam on beyond Finn's view into the dimness of the deep. A trail of bubbles was all that remained.

Finn woke up to the sound of someone saying, "Wake up! Wake up, it's only a dream!" It was Olaf shaking him by the shoulder. Finn blinked at him. The stars were there, rocking in the sky, and the creak and groan of the ship.

"Go back to sleep now, Reckless Skald," said Olaf in a soft tone.

At last the headlands of home appeared like a line of clouds on the horizon. A few sentinel icebergs held to the north and the pack ice appeared like a line of low breakers far beyond. They'd been lucky to beat the ice. The breeze held fair and *Sea Sword* coasted through the outlying skerries into the inlet. They skirted small bergs and patches of solid ice. Leif held the tiller and Finn stood up at the bow, watching the familiar shores of Greenland take on shape.

When Olaf joined him, Finn said, "Father, I've been

thinking. Remember when you said that someday the sunstone would be my eyes?"

"I do. It was before we sailed for Wineland."

"Yes, and you were right. But I know now there's more to seeing than using a sunstone. The things I need to see, no sunstone can show me. Do you understand?"

"I do, Finn. You need to see within yourself."

"Yes, and you've helped me. But there's something else."

"What's that?"

"Leif could use the sunstone. I would like to show my gratitude to him. I would like to give it to him as a gift." He reached into his tunic and took out the pouch. He opened it and shook the sunstone into the palm of his hand.

"Finn, the decision is yours. And for what it's worth, I think it's a wise one."

"Thank you, Father," he said, replacing the sunstone. He walked aft.

"Leif, the sunstone has served us well," he said. "I want to thank you for all you've done for me. Please take the sunstone as my gift to you. No more will you need to rely on ravens to help you navigate."

Father was right, thought Finn. The sunstone did turn out to be my eyes.

Leif took the pouch, began to speak, then made a small bow.

"Thank you," he said.

Olaf stepped onto the afterdeck to join them.

"Father," said Finn. "Look. We're almost home." The headlands, the cove, and the low buildings were coming into view.

When he looked into his father's face, he could see tears in his eyes.

Olaf reached a hand up and gripped his son by the shoulder.

Finn looked across the gleaming water to see the figures of the villagers running down to the beach to greet them. His heart was dancing in his chest. Wulf stood beside him, whimpering with excitement, and nudged his hand with his nose.

Sea Sword skimmed across the water, and soon Finn could make out the figures on the beach. Yes, there was old Floki, up in his lookout perch. There was Bo, white hair streaming behind him as he raced along the beach. And there was Freydis, walking toward the water, her honey-colored hair glinting in the sunlight.

But where was his mother?

All the Vikings lined the rails. But they did not dance or clap each other on the back or shout to the villagers. This was not their village. These were not their people. Only a few of the men offered a sheepish wave.

At last his mother appeared, running down the path

the way she had so long ago. She stopped at the water's edge. He could see her clap her hands. Then from around a bend in the path old Rollo appeared, hobbling up to her as fast as he could. His mother brought her hands to her face.

The gulls wheeled above the ship and cried their piercing cries, their shadows knifing across the deck. And with the shadows a chill rippled through him. He now noticed how quiet the villagers were as they watched the ship draw near. He understood their silence. They were watching a ship return, it was true, but it was only *Sea Sword.* Of the fifteen Vikings who'd set sail on *Dragonwing,* only two were coming home. Their loved ones remained behind in Wineland.

His mother stood off to the side, watching the ship come in, not yet knowing the fate of one of her sons.

He felt his father's firm grip on his shoulder, and he turned to look at him.

"We've made it home, Finn," said Olaf, his mouth set in a hard line. "We're the lucky ones. Now we must begin building a new *Dragonwing,* and set sail once again."

Finn looked back at his mother on the beach. The dog stood by her side, as Wulf stood by him. She touched a hand to her hair, then clasped her hands in front of her as if she did not know what to do with them. Then she let a hand drift to the top of the dog's head, and she ruffled his fur.

As Finn let his hand stroke Wulf's fur, and *Sea Sword* slipped to shore, a poem of shadow and light, hardship and laughter, sorrow and triumph set sail in his heart.